HOPE

IS LIKE A ROAD
IN THE COUNTRY:
THERE WAS NEVER A
ROAD, BUT WHEN MANY
PEOPLE WALK ON IT, THE
ROAD COMES INTO EXISTENCE.

From *The Epigrams of Lusin,* translated by Lin Yutang

THE
WAY
BACK
FROM
BROKEN

AMBER J. KEYSER

♦ carolrhoda LAB
MINNEAPOLIS

Carolrhoda Lab™
An imprint of Carolrhoda Books
A division of Lerner Publishing Group, Inc.
241 First Avenue North
Minneapolis, MN 55401 USA

For reading levels and more information, look up this title at www.lernerbooks.com.

Front cover and interior photographs: © Nine OK/Photographer's Choice/Getty Images (canoe); © Todd Strand/Independent Picture Service (paddle).

Main body text set in Janson Text LT Std 10.5/15.
Typeface provided by Linotype AG.

Library of Congress Cataloging-in-Publication Data

Keyser, Amber.
    The way back from broken / by Amber J. Keyser.
        pages cm
        Summary: "After losing his infant sister, Rakmen's family is devastated. While his parents figure things out, they send Rakmen on a camping trip in the Canadian wilderness with another grieving family. Rakmen is far from thrilled about the trip, and he has to decide whether it's too late to find his way back from broken"
    —Provided by publisher.
        ISBN 978-1-4677-7590-8 (lb : alk. paper)
        ISBN 978-1-4677-8817-5 (eb pdf : alk. paper)
        [1. Grief—Fiction. 2. Death—Fiction. 3. Brothers and sisters—Fiction.
    4. Camping—Fiction. 5. Survival—Fiction. 6. Racially mixed people—Fiction.
    7. Canada—Fiction.] I. Title.
    PZ7.1.K513Way 2015
    [Fic]—dc23   2015001617

Manufactured in the United States of America
2 – BP – 11/1/15

FOR SETH,
WHO CROSSED
EVERY PORTAGE
AND HELPED
CARRY THE LOAD

CHAPTER 1

On the way to Promise House, Rakmen sat in the backseat. His father drove, both hands gripping the wheel, while his mother brooded out the window. An ambulance screamed by on Lombard, sending up spray from puddles of spring rain. Rakmen winced and looked away, but the piercing red lights flooded the inside of the car.

Outside, night was coming fast.

Inside, the silence between his parents was louder than the siren.

When they stopped at the next light, a missing boy stared at him from a poster tacked to a telephone pole. Rakmen rolled down the window, squinting at the water-stained picture. The boy wore glasses and a crooked grin. Rakmen leaned out so he could read every word of the fading text.

He felt his mother turn toward him and rolled up the window before she could complain about the rain coming in. As his dad accelerated through the intersection, Rakmen fumbled in his pocket for a battered notebook. He scrawled the details about the disappeared kid. *Eight years old. Blond. Last seen wearing a red t-shirt and jeans. Over a year ago.* Not gonna be a happy ending to that story. He had to remember that.

They pulled to a stop in front of a large gray house with a wrap-around porch. A purple-flowered vine had the railing in a stranglehold. It was too nice a house for such a crappy neighborhood. Even the bathrooms at the Safeway down the block were code-locked.

The engine went silent. No one moved.

Finally, his mother cleared her throat. "Michael, are you sure you won't come?"

In the back seat, Rakmen tensed.

"Mercedes—" His dad's voice was gentle as he said her name, but it held ten months of the same disagreement.

"Alright, alright. I know," she said, reaching for his hand on the steering wheel and lacing her fingers through his much darker ones. "I just think it would be good for you."

If only Rakmen could get out so easily. Group scab-picking was not his idea of fun.

"I'm going to have a beer with Ray," said his dad. "I'll pick you up at eight fifteen."

Rakmen's mom nodded, released his hand, and opened the car door. "Come on, Rakmen."

He tugged at the collar of his church shirt but didn't move. "I don't need to come here any more."

She cleared her throat again, refusing to look at him.

Ten months. Ten shitty, pointless months he'd been coming here with her. He was fifteen. Old enough to know what wasn't working.

"You're coming."

Rakmen nudged his dad on the shoulder. "I could hang out with you guys."

"Go with your mother," he said, staring straight ahead.

Rakmen got out of the car, cursing under his breath. No one was ever on his side. Not that he blamed them. Even as he slammed the car door and let himself be swallowed by the dismal house, he knew there were some things that couldn't be forgiven.

Once inside the bolted front entry, his mother joined the parents' support group in the formal parlor where the therapist, whose name he never remembered, slid chairs into an expectant circle. The moms—and they were always moms, never dads because those guys chose beer over this train wreck—slumped into rockers and armchairs.

Rakmen's sneakers squeaked on the gleaming, lemon-scented wood floor as he headed toward the basement, where an art therapy intern waited with tubs of paint and markers and "feeling words."

At the top of the stairs, the therapist stopped him with one hand on his arm. She was so tiny he could see the graying roots on the top of her head. She wore a ring on every finger, even her thumbs.

"Hey, Tall Boy," she said, smiling like height was an accomplishment. "Do you mind getting some tissue boxes down?" She gestured to a closet in the hall. "They're on the top shelf."

He nodded, pulled down six boxes of Kleenex and left her to put one in reach of every arm. Behind him the security buzzer at the door whined like an angry hornet.

"I'll get it," Rakmen said. Anything to avoid the basement, where he'd spend the next hour half-choked by memories that wouldn't stay where they belonged.

Behind the rain-streaked windows, Molly and her mother stood shoulder to shoulder. Their pale faces and blond hair swam in the distorted glass, disembodied against the dark outside. Like most of the other white ladies who ventured into North Portland for group, Molly's mother, Kate, glanced nervously over one shoulder, clutching her handbag straps.

She used to look at him that way.

Rakmen knew what she saw. He was as tall as his dad but skinnier and not as dark. Both his hair and skin tended toward his Mexican mother. He hid, sullen and growly, under his too-long hair all the time. Once Kate had probably thought he looked dangerous, but inexplicably, she'd decided months ago that he was safe for Molly, and that was all that mattered. She side-hugged him, waved weakly at Molly, and went to join the other moms in the parlor full of Kleenexes.

"Hey," said Molly, smiling up at him as she peeled off her rain coat. A damp strand of hair stuck to the starburst scar on her left temple, an everyday reminder of the crash that killed her sister.

But she was still pretty. Really pretty.

Molly held up a Whole Foods shopping bag. "Snacks."

They met up here and only here, in this misfit jumble of rich and poor, religious and not, white and brown, where everyone came in pairs. Molly and her dead sister. Him and Dora. They were damaged goods who knew each other's secrets.

Well, most of them.

Last summer, he'd run into Molly and some of her friends at the Alberta Street Fair. That was awkward as all get-out. His buddies from school still wouldn't shut up about "Blondie." They didn't get it. Promise House was not a place for girlfriends.

The buzzer rang again.

"I'll meet you downstairs," said Molly, her arm skimming his as she went.

Rakmen opened the door and grunted hello to D'Vareay and D'Mareay. The twins were a year behind him at Roosevelt, fellow inmates of the north end of the city. The boys' mom, a woman built like a linebacker, lumbered to the parlor in silence.

It was a little after seven o'clock. Group was starting, but Rakmen lingered in the foyer, watching the drizzle. A homeless man trundled by, pushing a shopping cart crammed with bundles swathed in a torn tarp. A rusty brown pit bull mix plodded behind him, nose nearly scraping the sidewalk. Rakmen crunched his lanky frame into the window seat and turned to a new page in the notebook. *Sleeping on the streets. In the rain. Under a blue plastic tarp. With a starving dog.*

Several more women showed up, each one exhausted and warped around the edges. Children clutched at their legs. Rakmen opened the door and watched as the women disentangled small arms and sent their offspring trotting downstairs. Hollowness pushed against his bones. The cover of the notebook tore as he crushed it between hands too big for the rest of him.

He wished he could un-see what he'd seen.

In the parlor, the meeting began in a tumbled murmur of voices.

One of the moms started to cry almost immediately. Rakmen hummed a monotone under his breath. Sometimes it felt like all he did was listen to sobbing.

A few minutes later, the door buzzer startled the group in the parlor into temporary silence. Rakmen looked up to see two more faces through the wavy glass. New members, he figured, since the regulars were all here. Rakmen unfolded his body from the window seat, opened the door, and gaped as fragments of his life collided.

"Uh . . . Mrs. Tatlas?" Rakmen asked. He peered from her pinched face, distorted by grief, to the chubby little girl next to her.

A wan, confused look washed over Mrs. Tatlas. "Rakmen?"

In one heartbeat, Rakmen knew exactly why she was here. Before winter break, his biology teacher had been pushing her pregnant belly through the halls like a wheelbarrow. When a deflated version of herself had rejoined the class two months later, he'd figured she'd had the baby like normal.

Guess not.

"So . . . are you here for the group?" he asked, forcing out the words.

Her muddy brown eyes searched the shiny foyer as if looking for some clue as to why she was standing there. The daughter peered at him through a fringe of dull brown bangs that skimmed her cheeks.

"Why are you here?" Mrs. Tatlas asked, fidgeting with the zipper on her purse.

"My mom comes." Rakmen pointed to the parlor. "Group's in there. Kids go downstairs."

The girl squeezed closer to her mother. Mrs. Tatlas seemed unsteady on her feet. Rakmen thought she might fall, but he couldn't bear to touch her. He stepped past them and pushed the front door closed, making sure it was locked.

Circling back, he addressed the girl. "Come on."

She didn't move.

"Um . . ." he began, turning to Mrs. Tatlas for guidance. "Do you want me to—"

"I got lost on the way here," she said.

He stared at her shoulder. A blotch of something stained the blue fabric of her sleeve. "It's okay," he said. "They're just getting started. Go on in."

Mrs. Tatlas shook her head as if clearing away a fog. "Where did you say the kids go?"

"Downstairs. With the art therapist. I'll show her."

His teacher looked down at her daughter as if she hardly recognized her. "Okay then. Be good, sweetie." She disentangled her hand from her daughter's grip and joined the other moms.

Rakmen crouched in front of the girl. "What's your name?"

"Jacey."

She was nine or ten with oversized front teeth and growing-out bangs that refused to stay behind her ears. Her gray eyes analyzed him from head to toe, as if checking for radioactivity.

"I don't bite," he said.

"I know that." She spat out the words. "I'm assessing damage."

Rakmen stood, held his arms out, and spun a slow, irritated circle as if showing off his outfit. "Satisfied?" he muttered.

She frowned, but apparently he'd passed some kind of test because she slipped her pudgy hand into his. "I'm ready now."

Her palm was warm and damp, and he did not want to be this close to anyone. Halfway down the stairs, his phone vibrated. Rakmen slipped from her grip and fished for it in his pocket.

"Head on down," he told Jacey.

She glared up at him. "You're supposed to stay with me."

He shooed her off and read the text from Juan. **How's Blondie?**

Jacey shot him another scowl and huffed down the stairs.

Blond, he texted back. They all needed to lay off this shit.

I'd like to get some of that.

Rakmen shoved the phone in his pocket. It had been ten months since the thought of a girl had even made him hard. Juan could keep on trying to get laid but not with Molly. Not ever with her. Juan wouldn't understand how her sister Rissa was still there, behind the scar on Molly's forehead, in the empty seat at the table.

From the parlor, he heard Mrs. Tatlas's voice.

"My name's Leah. I . . . um . . . I was pregnant." A soft murmur rose from the other women. He did not, did not, did not want to hear this. No amount of Kleenex or therapy circles or talking would change anything.

Rakmen closed the basement door and slumped down the stairs, avoiding eye contact as he stepped into the low-ceilinged room. The formal upstairs made Rakmen feel out of place, but downstairs matched him exactly, from the stained shag carpet to the torn pool table. The buzzing white fluorescents almost always smothered the crying upstairs.

And then there were the others, his sort-of-friends. After months of trying not to know their names and stories, he had learned them anyway. At least he knew the bits and pieces dragged out of them by Keri, the art therapist, who smiled too widely and gestured him toward the cast-off school tables clustered in the middle of the room.

"You're here," she said as if that were cause for celebration.

The twins, big as grown men, sat shoulder to shoulder on kid-sized school chairs. They bent over a short-legged table, inking their names in tagger lettering on its edge. D'Vareay wore cornrows and D'Mareay had his head shaved to almost nothing, but otherwise they were identical from their empty expressions to the matching tattoos on the napes of their necks.

D'Shawn—Never Forget.

Molly sat across from them, flanked by two younger girls who had her drawing unicorns. Her eyes flicked up and met Rakmen's. The look was both a secret handshake and a plea. Molly was quicksand-trapped sure as the rest of them. Since the crash, her parents' hyper-vigilance had gone through the roof. Molly hadn't been let out alone in a year.

Jacey sat separated from the rest, sucking on a lock of hair like her life depended on it and staring at him.

"Well," said Keri, extricating herself from the huddle of little ones playing with hand-me-down toys in one corner. "Shall we get started?"

Rakmen could hardly wait.

The twins covered their graffiti with a piece of art paper. Molly pulled herself to attention, trying too hard as usual. Rakmen knew the drill, but falling in step didn't help. It never got better.

Keri spread out markers, paints, colored pencils and modeling clay. "I thought we'd start with a really open-ended statement: *I feel the most in charge when. . .* You can address it in writing or visually, if you want." The moms upstairs got Kleenex; the kids downstairs got art supplies. In the end, it all wound up in the trash.

"We can talk too," said Keri, nodding encouragingly at each of them.

Nobody said anything.

Keri was always trying for meaningful conversation. It made Rakmen's stomach churn. Their perky therapist was the only one in the room who didn't walk with the dead day in and day out. She was woefully ill-equipped to facilitate anything.

"Well, you know what I always say," Keri said to the silent room. "Words are short, but art is long. Let's draw."

"Art is a pain in the ass," Rakmen muttered, burying his nose in the newspaper that Keri brought to protect the table. He jotted headlines in his notebook. *Broke rancher leaves 120 horses to starve in the Wallowas. Flood of toxic sludge engulfs town in Hungary. Coast Guard abandons search for three fishermen missing on the Columbia Bar.*

"Doing some writing, Rakmen?" Keri asked, leaning over his shoulder.

He slid a hand over the page.

She backed off as if he'd bitten her. "Private, I know."

He wrote things down to remember. Forgetting was dangerous. Bad stuff kept coming, and you had to brace for it. He pulled the itchy collar away from his neck.

Keri sat down by Jacey and got sized up and down. "So your mom is probably having a really hard time, isn't she?"

Jacey nodded.

D'Vareay rolled his eyes at Rakmen and went back to drawing

bloody knives wreathed in black roses. From the fine spray of colored paint on the thighs of both boys' jeans, he figured they'd already found their artistic outlet for the day.

"The group upstairs," Keri said to Jacey, "it will be good for your mom. Talking about things—and time—that's what helps."

Molly gave Rakmen a wan smile. That particular lie was as much a part of the Promise House basement as the buzzing fluorescent lights and the ugly carpet. They could sit here forever and nothing would change.

"What are you going to draw?" Keri asked Jacey, ever persistent. "When do you feel in charge?"

"I'm a kid," said Jacey, her voice flat, her face blank. "I'm never in charge."

"Well . . .," Keri gulped. "I'm sure you can . . . just . . . draw something. Your favorite animal?"

Jacey put the sodden lock of hair back in her mouth and stared at Keri until she turned away. Then Jacey stood and picked up her chair. For a moment Rakmen thought she might throw it. Instead she carried it around the table and wedged in next to his. He turned to the obits, ignoring her.

An undulating wail from upstairs fractured the uneasy pause.

Even the little ones bickering over toys in the corner fell silent. Jacey shifted closer to Rakmen. Keri gasped, froze. So much for her being in charge.

The crying rose a notch, and Molly shot a pleading look at Rakmen. Do something, she mouthed.

His limbs were leaden, but he pushed back from the table. If he could help anyone, which he doubted he could, he would want to help Molly. He turned on the crappy old dehumidifier, which rattled even louder than the lights buzzed, muffling the sounds from upstairs. It was the best he could do.

Exhaustion poured through Rakmen. This day needed to end. But when he turned back to the group, they were all watching him. He leaned against the wall and tipped his head back to avoid their eyes.

Every day ended like this, and every day he wondered how he could survive another one.

"Here's the deal," he said, talking to the ceiling tiles. "We're all in a club no one wants to join. We hang out. Our moms cry."

Jacey whimpered like a kicked dog.

"At least here, everybody knows you're missing something."

"Like a leg?" Jacey asked, her need for answers a gaping wound.

Keri opened and closed her mouth like a fish. The worthless woman was swimming in the wrong pool, but Rakmen knew exactly what Jacey meant. "Yeah, it's exactly like you're missing a leg, but no one can see that it's gone."

The stuffy basement was suddenly crammed full of the dead. Molly was digging her nails into the soft flesh of her upper arms. The girl next to her blacked out the unicorn drawing in long steady strokes with a Sharpie. The twins looked ready to break the table in half. The little ones playing blocks began to cry.

"How do we walk?" Jacey whispered.

Even though he could barely hear her, Rakmen felt her question in his bones. He thought he might sink through the floor into the heavy earth. Maybe then he could rest.

The girl started to sob. She was looking to him for answers he didn't have.

"I don't know," he pleaded, "with a limp, I guess."

CHAPTER 2

Even after Rakmen retreated to his room that night, the girl's question gnawed at him. She'd burrowed into things he kept tucked away and expected him to have answers.

He didn't have answers.

He didn't have anything.

Rakmen flicked off the light, abandoning the pretense of studying for tomorrow's biology test. Once he'd dreamed of architecture school. At this rate, he'd be lucky to finish high school. It was all so much empty effort.

The dishwasher gurgled in the kitchen downstairs. The orange glow of the street light illuminated the room, stripped to the bare essentials—twin bed, black desk, straight-backed chair. The stuff Rakmen used to care about—scale models of bridges and posters of snowboarders—were in a landfill somewhere. Tenuous heights and steep slopes made him think of snapped necks and shattered skulls. He hadn't been to the mountain since Dora died.

Rakmen slid into bed and pulled a pillow over his head to block the noise of traffic. When he finally slept, he dreamed of biology— deformed frogs and genetic mutations.

"*¡Despiértate!*" His mother shook him awake.

He couldn't have been asleep more than a few minutes.

"Huh? What?" Rakmen fumbled for the clock—almost midnight. "Yeah?"

Illuminated by traces of orange light from outside, she sat in his desk chair, cell phone muffled against her chest. The strain on her face brought him fully awake, chest thudding.

He sat up. "What is it? What's wrong?"

She shook her head, "I don't know. There's a little girl on the phone and says she has to talk to you."

"Who?" he asked, rubbing his temples.

"Jacey. Your biology teacher's daughter."

His head was thick with sleep. The gears turned slowly. Jacey. The girl from the basement. "What's she want?"

"She won't talk to me. Says it has to be you."

"How does she even have your number?"

"I gave it to her mom after group last night." She held out the phone.

He squinted against the screen's blue light and started to lie back down. "She needs to talk to you. Not me."

"*¡Tomalo!*" His mother whispered the command. He shook his head. She tugged on his blanket and pushed the phone toward him. Every part of her body said *you will talk to her*.

Rakmen sat back up. "Fine."

His mother sat back down in the desk chair.

"Hello?"

A long-held breath whooshed through the phone, followed by a sob. "It's you," she said, her voice sounding younger than he remembered. Another deep breath. "Make it stop," she wailed, loud enough for his mom to hear.

"What are you talking about?"

A series of breathy hiccups came through the phone. He waited. More hiccups. He yawned again, squeezing the bridge of his nose with a free hand and extending the phone to his mother. He needed to sleep, not talk to a messed-up little girl.

A tremendous crash exploded through the phone. Both Rakmen

and his mother jumped. He snapped the phone back to his ear in time to hear another crash.

Jacey gulped like a drowning girl. "My mom's crying and breaking plates."

Rakmen's mom raised her eyebrows in question.

Another plate hit the wall.

"So your mom's really missing the baby tonight," he said, not bothering to make it a question. The answer was loud enough.

"Uh huh," said Jacey. "And . . . and . . ." The words were traffic-jamming in her mouth. "Rakmen . . ."

"Yeah?"

"My dad's at work and . . . " Another plate shattered. " . . . and she's trapped!"

For a split second, Rakmen thought of calling 911. They needed professional help. Someone other than him. But there was no fixing what was wrong in that family.

He knew that from experience.

"You have to make her understand." Jacey's voice shook. "I didn't mean anything bad."

"What did you do?" Fear rose in Rakmen. He knew how unstable grief could make parents.

"I dreamed about Jordan—that's my baby—and us and you. And we were all okay. We were someplace sunny."

"Then what?"

"I woke up and told her about it."

Rakmen covered his face with one hand. "You shouldn't have—"

Another crash. There wouldn't be any plates left.

"You have to talk to her."

"I can't."

"You can."

"It's the middle of the—"

"I'll take the phone to her." On the other end of the line, he could hear Jacey getting up from wherever she was sitting. Another plate shattered. Rakmen was wide awake now. He imagined the star-like

13

explosion frozen in mid-fall for the space between heartbeats, and then the shards clattered to the floor.

"Wait!" he shouted and heard her sit back down again. "Jacey-girl. I can't—"

Jacey cut him off. "You can! I had a dream!"

"Hey, why don't you talk to my mom for a while? She's good with this stuff. You know, she's been there."

"But I had a dream!"

"Jacey, Martin Luther King had a goddamn dream. You had a nightmare. So did your mom."

"My baby brother was not a nightmare!" she shrieked.

Rakmen held the phone away from his ear. Jacey's screech transformed into wild, rolling sobs. He had nothing for her. There was no stopping the plates. Rakmen handed the phone to his mom and pulled the covers over his head.

The wet warmth of his own breath filled the claustrophobic space under the blankets. He heard his mother crooning something soft and soothing. He willed her to leave.

Jacey howled his name as if she could drag him to her through the phone. Rakmen flattened his hands against his ears and listened to the rush of his own blood. From inside the cave of blankets, Rakmen heard the distant shattering of one more plate before the call ended. He held his breath and waited for his mom to get up and go.

Instead, she tore away the covers. "Come on."

"You can't be serious."

She made one of those faces.

"We don't know them. We don't even know where they live."

"*La señora* was in group tonight. That's all I need to know." His mom's voice was hard. "They live close."

"You're crazy," Rakmen muttered, groping for the blankets.

"Oh no, you don't. You're coming with me. I don't know what is going on over there, but that little girl wants you. You know I know where her mama is right now. Let's go."

"You can't be serious."

"*Si, mijo*. Get dressed. *¡Ahorita!*" She flicked the overhead light on as she left the room.

He groaned and slid out of bed. When she spoke Spanish, you pretty much had to do what she said. As Rakmen pulled on his jeans, he stumbled into the desk and sent his biology folder crashing. His notes scattered across the floor. Nothing good would come of this.

. . .

Pelting raindrops glowed in the halogen lights of the Plaid Pantry on the corner as his mom parked in front of a boxy, brown house. Dandelions and crabgrass grew in the cracks crisscrossing the front walk. A single pot of pansies was on the front step.

"Can't I wait in the car?"

"No," his mom snapped.

"She's my teacher. This is weird."

"The little girl wants you."

"Why?"

"She can tell you're a kind person."

Rakmen ducked his head, breath in his throat. His mom might as well have punched him.

"Let's go," she said, propelling him out of the car and up to the door. Rakmen hung back, slouched against the rain, while she knocked, waited, and knocked harder.

"Leah!" she called through the door. "It's me. Mercedes. From Promise House."

The solid door squealed open a crack. Mrs. Tatlas's pale face seemed to float in the dim light. The plate crashing and crying had done a job on her. She looked like a wadded-up paper towel. One white-knuckled hand clenched the door frame. Her eyes darted between them. "What are you doing here?"

"Jacey called," said his mother, trying to squeeze under the eaves and out of the rain. The barely contained hysteria in Mrs. Tatlas repelled Rakmen. He stood as far back as he could. An icy finger of rain snaked down his neck, and he shivered.

"I don't know what you're talking about."

His mom shrugged and ventured a half-smile. "I guess she found my number in your phone and seemed to think that you might need someone to talk to."

"And you came in the middle of the night?" Disbelief laced her words. "You both came?"

His mom shrugged again, and Rakmen fought the urge to bolt to the car and lock the doors behind him. Jacey slid into view behind her mother, eyes fixed on Rakmen's face like tractor beams. He stepped back involuntarily, wanting to move out of range.

"Can we come in?" his mom asked.

Mrs. Tatlas swayed slightly. "I don't . . . It's really late."

But Jacey pulled the door open wide.

Mrs. Tatlas was in her pajamas. Under the thin blue T-shirt, Rakmen could see the outline of her breasts. The flannel bottoms were torn in one knee, and he could see flesh there too. She was like a body at a crime scene, no longer capable of modesty. He wanted to cover her with a sheet. Instead he looked away.

Mrs. Tatlas stepped aside for them to enter, shut the door behind them and turned on Jacey. "What have you done?" The girl hid behind those scraggly bangs. She wore a patterned nightgown. Dogs or rabbits. An animal of some kind. Her bare feet unnerved him.

"Look," said his mom. "It's no big deal. Everybody needs somebody to talk to sometimes."

Mrs. Tatlas lifted her hands, and for a second Rakmen thought she might slap Jacey, but instead her arms dropped to her sides, too heavy to hold. "My husband, George, is working tonight, and I—"

"Come on. Got any tea?" Rakmen's mom guided Mrs. Tatlas into her own kitchen, leaving Rakmen and Jacey in the dark entry hall.

He sat down on the staircase. The carpet between his feet was stained. Something dark. Something old. Another family's mess. Next to him, Jacey's fingers crumpled and uncrumpled the fabric of her nightgown against her thighs. He could hear the faint, wet sound of her chewing on her hair.

In the kitchen, the faucet went on then off. The kettle went on the burner with a metallic clunk, followed by the whoosh of gas. "Broom?" his mother murmured. A moment later, he heard bristles on linoleum and the clatter of porcelain shards. Things break and go in the trash. And he was always overhearing.

"I'm sorry she called you," said Mrs. Tatlas.

"Hard night?"

Beside him, Jacey's breathing was fast and shallow.

"You should go back to bed," he told her.

Jacey shook her head. She was not a pretty girl. Not the kind who got her cheeks pinched. Not like Dora, whom he'd watched sleep, her lips moving in that other-worldly baby way. Not like Dora, who had been beautiful.

Jacey shifted next to him, her bare feet shuffling against the ratty carpet. A nondescript, unremarkable girl in a crumbling house.

The kitchen voices rose.

"One of the girls in my fifth period class had a baby boy last night."

"Dios mío."

"And he's fine!" Mrs. Tatlas's voice cranked up. "She's sixteen. Smokes cigarettes. Drinks Red Bull. Eats like crap. Her baby's fine and mine's . . ." The volume dropped, muffled by tears.

Marissa.

Rakmen knew she did worse than smoke cigarettes, much worse. Juan had screwed her at a party where they were all doing crank and tequila shots, back when it didn't seem possible that they could mess things up very bad.

"We'd tried for a long time after Jacey was born," said Mrs. Tatlas. "We really wanted two. And Jacey—that little goose has been begging for a baby brother practically since she could talk."

Next to him, Jacey started to cry.

It was always this. Women crying. Men leaving. Him overhearing.

17

Rakmen stood up. "Come on," he told Jacey. "Let's go upstairs. I'll read you a story or something."

She wiped her eyes on her sleeve and padded up the stairs. Jacey passed the doorway to her room where the pink glow of a lava lamp oozed across the walls and the green safari net over her bed billowed in a blast of hot air from the floor vent. Instead, she opened the door of the nursery. Blue walls, freshly-painted. Rocking chair. A painting of Noah's Ark in bright colors.

Rakmen hung back. "Let's go to your room and find a book."

Jacey ran her finger along the crib rail. "This was mine when I was a baby, but we lived in a different house."

A teddy bear slumped next to a carefully folded quilt on an unwrinkled sheet. This room had never seen spit-up or dirty diapers or late-night feedings. It smelled like fabric softener and the sterile aisles at Babies-R-Us.

It did not smell like baby.

Rakmen picked at the torn lining of his jacket pocket, trying not to remember Dora's sweet, milky breath.

Downstairs, Mrs. Tatlas's voice rose again, fractured and staccato.

Rakmen stepped inside, shut the nursery door behind him, and leaned against it, heaviness sucking him down. Jacey lifted a wooden chest the size of a shoe box from the end of the crib and carried it to the rocking chair. When she sat, her feet didn't touch the ground.

"Shouldn't he feel close?" she asked, clasping the box to her chest. "It's only been a few months. I thought he'd hang around. But I don't feel him at all. That's why the dream made me happy. Because Jordan was with us. And Mom was happy. I thought she'd want to know."

Rakmen dropped his head to his chest. Dreams were empty cribs and unused bedrooms. "She's upset about the girl at school," he said.

"I know." Jacey stretched one toe to the floor and rocked herself in the chair. The wood creaked rhythmically.

"What's in the box?"

"My brother's ashes. Wanna see them?" She went to open the lid.

"No!" Rakmen snapped.

Jacey shut it and glared at him. "Fine. I'll show you his picture instead."

She put the box back in the crib, patted it softly, and tucked the stuffed bear in next to it. She gestured for him to come to the changing table by the window. Rakmen pushed off the door and crossed the room to her. Morning was only a few hours away. He needed sleep before he had to get through another day.

On the changing table, Jacey had arranged a series of objects. She touched them one by one. "Jordan's rattle. Mom's hospital bracelet—I saved it from the trash. And look at this list." She crinkled a piece of paper in front of his nose. It held a list of names written in misshapen, fourth grade print: *Jonah, Benjamin (Ben), Samuel, Max, Martin, Jordan.* The last name on the list was circled in pink marker, and she'd drawn little hearts around it.

"When we picked the name, Mom and Dad and I had a party with cupcakes. Dad said he wasn't going to be outnumbered anymore." She took back the list and replaced it near a tiny pair of mint green socks and one of those bulbs for sucking snot out of baby noses.

"Here," said Jacey, holding out a piece of stiff paper.

He didn't want to take it.

She shook it at him, frowning.

He took it. The certificate was from the hospital. *Jordan Timothy Tatlas. Weight 6 lbs 11 ounces. Stillborn December 21.* There were two footprints. The left slightly turned in. A wispy chunk of brown hair was taped below the photo of the baby's slightly squashed newborn face, eyes squeezed shut, lips the color of dried blood.

"I don't know why his lips are so dark," she said quietly, taking back the picture. "Was your baby like that?"

Rakmen jumped away like she'd bitten him, pressing his back against the door.

Jacey stared at him, her eyes huge and almost round like the luminous eyes on some deep-sea fish. The drumming of his own pulse was louder than the rain on the thin roof.

"Well," asked Jacey. "Was she? Or he?"

His breath came faster.

"She." Rakmen choked on the word.

The girl smiled a little, like she was meeting his sister for the first time, like this was normal conversation. But normal people knew better than to ask questions like that. Normal people didn't keep ashes in a dead baby's room. Normal men pretended nothing had happened.

Exhaustion rolled over him.

Jacey pinned him with her eyes. "Was she born dead?"

"No." His answer barely escaped his constricted throat.

"When did she die?"

He scowled at her.

"It's a fair question."

He was not talking about this.

"What was your sister's name?"

The guttural growl that escaped him drove her cowering into the corner. Scared of what he might do, Rakmen slid to the floor, his head in his hands. On the other side of the room, he could hear her crying.

"Why'd you call me?" he demanded.

She was crying harder now, but he couldn't muster a shred of kindness. Anger was a whip coiled in his chest. His voice rose. "Why did you call me?"

"To help us," she whispered.

Rakmen twitched against the door like he'd been skewered. He couldn't even save himself. "You don't know me."

"I know enough," Jacey said, "because of what you said about the leg." She paused, picked up the teddy bear. "Can you see them too?"

"See who?" he asked, but he already knew. Of course he could see them. Every time he walked down the street, he could pick them out. Strangers limping along. Invisible amputees. Their pain palpable.

"Rakmen?" His mom's voice flew up the stairs like a rescue rope. He shot from the room, fled to the car, and slammed the door behind him. Panting and wiping the rain from his face, he bent almost double against the seething ache in his gut. He squeezed his eyes shut, blocking out the night, the house, everything.

Only after his mother had started the car and had begun to pull away from the curb did he look back. In the upstairs window, Jacey's round face glowed like a moon. The house seemed as if it might come apart like a wet cardboard box.

His hands shook as he opened the notebook.

There are no plates left.

The crib is empty.

Lips.

CHAPTER 3

Rakmen shuffled into the kitchen and blindly poured cereal into a bowl. The alarm clock had been an ice pick to the temple.

"Morning," said his mom as she measured coffee into the pot.

He grunted and slumped into a chair on his side of the table, the side that kept his back to the pictures on the wall. Dora coming home, baby-fro sticking out all over. Dora asleep on his dad's chest like a golden brown loaf of bread in a diaper. Dora nestled in Rakmen's arms, her heart-shaped face beaming up at him.

"You have a test today?"

He nodded, scarfing breakfast.

She pulled coffee mugs from the cupboard. "I checked your grades online."

Rakmen froze with the spoon halfway to his mouth.

His mom turned to face him and crossed her arms over her chest.

He glared at her. She was all brittle edges, but he was too tired to care. "Yeah, I know. Mr. Ruben is a jerk, and your new best friend, Mrs. Tatlas, hasn't given a fair test all year."

His mom's eyes narrowed. "You've got a month to get them up."

Rakmen's dad came in, interrupting the mutual glare fest. "He'll take care of business. Won't you, son?" When some smart aleck at school heard that his dad was a nurse, they always flipped a load of crap. At least until they got a look at him. Before nursing school, he'd been a medic in the army. Biggest guy in the ER.

"I was up all night because of that idiot teacher."

His mom was half out of her chair before his dad intercepted, eased her back down into the chair, and began to knead her shoulders. "Calm down, sweetie. Rakmen's tired, that's all. I'm sure he'll pull it out of the bag. Right?" He raised an eyebrow at Rakmen. It was a look full of lifelines, red and white rings exchanged as if two drowning people could rescue each other.

"Yeah. Sure, Dad," he said. "Gotta run so I'm not late for school."

"And I've got to get all crazy with the bed pans."

It was an old joke that reminded Rakmen of a time when laughter came easily to all of them. "Bye, Mom," he said, pecking her on the cheek and bolting for the door before she could say anything else.

• • •

A pack of girls in low, tight pants were talking about Marissa's baby as Rakmen shoved his way through the front door at school.

"I heard Tyrone showed up at the hospital," said one.

"Yeah, and Marissa's mom screamed at him for getting her knocked up," said a blond girl. "They had to call security."

"But you know what?" This was a short, round girl with hoop earrings so large that Rakmen was pretty sure poodles could leap through them. "She named the baby Tyrone Jr."

"Bet her mama flipped out."

That girl didn't know crap about mothers flipping out.

"Hey, man," said Juan, catching up with him. "You ready for this test?"

Rakmen shoved his backpack into his locker. "Not even a little."

"Shoot. Same here."

They pushed through the crowded halls. His stomach twitched in anticipation of whatever hell awaited him inside. The test wouldn't go well. No surprise there. Chromosomal defects. Heritable disease. Pedigrees. It was all a blur. Mrs. Tatlas in the middle of the night. He'd been in her house. Seen her in goddamn pajamas.

"We missed you at the pickup game last night," said Juan as they slid into biology a few minutes before the bell. She wasn't there yet. He had a few minutes left to breathe. "You know," said Juan, nudging him to get his attention, "you could come back and play with us."

Rakmen shrugged and sat by the far windows.

"Suit yourself but I don't see why you ditched us."

"Didn't ditch you."

"You haven't come for a game in almost a year." Juan frowned at him. "That's called ditching, asshole."

The rest of the class rumbled in, the girls shrill and the guys loud. Rakmen's head was already pounding from lack of sleep, and even on a good day, school was like being bludgeoned with a hundred radios all set on different stations.

"You know," said Juan, scanning the classroom shelves full of animal skeletons, mounted birds, and stuff in jars. "This class used to be kinda cool. Remember how Mrs. T was all gaga into squid and photosynthesis and crap? She turned lame lately. You notice that?"

Rakmen wanted to puke. Instead, he shook his head. "Nah. Always sucked."

"Amen, brother. Here's to going down in flames."

Since there wasn't any point cramming for the test, Rakmen pulled the Metro section of the morning paper out of his backpack and got out his notebook. *Site of former meth lab contaminates local well. African-American church damaged by arson. Gray whale calf washes up near Newport.*

Juan leaned over. "Why do you keep all that downer stuff?"

Rakmen slid the notebook under the newspaper. He couldn't explain how bad news tacked him to the ground, how it kept him unsurprisable. Juan wouldn't understand.

The roar in the room settled when Mrs. Tatlas came in.

Rakmen kept his eyes glued to his desk.

"Quiet, everyone. You know the drill." Her voice was worn thin like the carpet in the basement of Promise House.

As the rest of the students cleared their desks, Rakmen retrieved his notebook and added one more line. Marissa.

Mrs. Tatlas began to distribute the stack of tests tucked under her arm. "This is your last unit test before the final in June, which is, I remind you, cumulative. So don't forget everything you learned for today." She didn't look at him when she passed.

Rakmen scanned the first page of the test. An essay on the evolutionary significance of mutation worth fifteen points.

"Bitch," Juan whispered to his desktop. "I hate long answer."

Rakmen skipped to the second page. He could feel Mrs. Tatlas up there at her desk sucking the air out of the room, and wanted to scream. Thanks to her, he hadn't slept. He was flunking for sure. And that girl—

Even now, Jacey clung to him. He could practically feel her sweaty hand squeezing his own hand numb. He could see her in the dim light of the nursery, box of ashes crushed against her chest.

Rabbits. They'd been rabbits on the fabric of her nightgown. Not dogs.

And now he couldn't forget that either.

Around him pencils scratched, and the second hand on the clock above the door lurched through each minute. At the front of the room, Jacey's mom sat woodenly, scanning for cheaters. Rakmen scattered *Fs and Ts* beside a series of statements without bothering to read them and scrawled in the short answers. The multiple choice section was pretty much as bad as he'd expected. With ten minutes left in the period, Rakmen flipped back to the essay. He kneaded his temples, trying to dredge up some crap answer for her.

Mutation is random changes to genes, he wrote. *Lots of times it happens in junk parts of DNA. Those mutations don't really matter. But when an important gene gets zapped, there's an opportunity.*

Uneasiness swept over Rakmen. When he looked over the bent backs of his classmates, Mrs. Tatlas was staring at him, dark smudges ringing her eyes, her skin pale and papery. She nodded sharply before dropping her eyes, and he was reminded of a emaciated bird.

It's not like the X-Men or anything where a mutation gives you super powers. That doesn't happen. Even those rare good mutations are kind of dumb—a better enzyme or curly fur or something like that.

Sometimes the animal dies. Other times it gets cancer or comes out deformed.

The textbook had shown color pictures of fruit flies with legs poking out where eyes should've been. Blind horses. Frogs with five legs.

It's usually bad. The weak die. That's natural selection.

During the autopsy, the doctors had measured Dora's malformed heart. It was twice the normal size from trying so hard to do its job.

Mutation made Darwin not believe in God.

CHAPTER 4

When Rakmen stepped into the basement at Promise House, Jacey super-glued herself to his side.

"I saved you a seat by me," she said, tugging on his arm.

In the month since she'd first showed up in the foyer, their moms had become friends. Mrs. Tatlas was everywhere. They drank coffee. They went for walks. They always left Jacey with him. Never asking. Always expecting. *Thanks for watching her, Rakmen. She loves you, Rakmen. You're the best, Rakmen.*

Jacey told every single person they met from checkout clerks to bus drivers that he was practically her adopted brother. She was like a puppy, always underfoot, but not nearly as cute.

Rakmen pulled free of Jacey's grasp and fist-bumped D'Mareay and D'Vareay, who were busy elaborating their tabletop graffiti. "What's up?"

"Not much," D'Mareay said. "Crazy white chick wants us to draw our support network." He pointed at Keri. Her butt was all they could see sticking out of the art supply cupboard.

"Yours is mainly skulls, huh?" said Rakmen, nodding at the table. "I can't believe she lets you do that, man."

"We're expressing ourselves," simpered D'Vareay in a terrible impression of the art therapist.

"We're like black Van Gogh over here," said his brother.

Rakmen noticed the traces of neon paint on D'Vareay's jeans and wondered where their real project was. "Don't cut off your ears."

D'Mareay replied with another Keri quote. "Art is long, man. Very long."

Rakmen pretended not to see Jacey's puppy eyes as he made his way to his spot on the puke-colored couch at the far end of the basement. Molly was already there, curled around her sketchbook. She didn't need Keri handing out assignments. She was always drawing.

"Hey you," she said, sweeping her hair out of her face and leaving a gray smudge of charcoal on her forehead. "How's tricks?"

"Tricky, I guess." He sat beside her and caught a whiff of strawberries. "Whatchya drawing?"

She held out the sketch pad.

A warped network of metal bars sprang directly from a meadow. Rakmen could practically feel the breeze whispering through the blades of tall grass. They rolled in gray-shaded waves across the paper. Amid all that rustling and growing, the cage Molly had drawn was fixed and immobile. He leaned closer, charcoal dust tickling his nose. The wind had pinned a moth inside the cage, pressing its tiny body against the bars.

"Whoa," he said. "It's really good but kinda scary."

Molly ducked her head, smiling. "I knew you'd get it, but don't tell my mom."

"Your secret's safe," said Rakmen, giving his shirt collar a tug, "but I don't think this is exactly what Keri had in mind with her little assignment."

"Tell me about it," Molly groaned. "I started with the meadow because I was thinking about how when I'm sad I like to walk in the arboretum near my house. But my parents won't let me go alone and then—poof—before I knew it I was drawing bars. Freud would have a field day with me."

Rakmen raised an eyebrow, stroked a pretend goatee, and in a wretched German accent said, "Tell me about your mother."

He'd meant to make her laugh, but instead her face fell, and she touched the scar on her temple. Her lower lip trembled, and scent of strawberry lip gloss wafted over him. Juan and the guys would ride him hard about that lip.

"There's this new girl at school who I've gotten to know," said Molly. "She's really nice." Rakmen watched her darken the shadows of the cage. "She was at my house yesterday, and we were talking about going to the Rose Festival Fun Center. My mom totally butted in and started going on about some girl who got decapitated on a roller coaster and another who was raped by a carnie and how the Rose Festival brings in all the meth heads from the east side . . ."

Molly's drawing pencil dug into the soft paper.

Rakmen laid his hand over hers. "You're going to ruin it."

She shrugged. "It's already ruined."

Rakmen wanted to say *I'm sorry* and *you're right* and *that sucks* all at the same time. He tried to smile in a way that said those things but probably looked like he had gas. He suddenly wanted to kiss the center of the scar that was not her fault. Instead, he pulled his hand away.

"She said we could go to the movies," said Molly, "as long as she drove and sat in the back of the theater. I could tell my friend thought she was totally creepy. I mean, who does that?"

"Dads afraid of boyfriends?"

"I know." Molly flopped back against the couch, face tilted to the ceiling.

Rakmen stared at the pulse in her neck. He wanted to catch it and hold it in his cupped hands. It would flutter there like a moth. He tore his eyes away from Molly and pulled out his notebook. *Cages. Carnies. One single moment is enough to change everything.*

"Hey." Jacey appeared in front of them, sucking furiously on a lock of hair. Without waiting for an invitation, she wormed her way between him and Molly on the couch. "Look at this," she said, patting the scrapbook she held in her lap. "Keri says it's a yearbook for dead babies."

Rakmen tried to prod her off the couch, but Molly scowled at him over Jacey's head, and he edged over to make space.

"It's a *memory* book, not a *year* book," Molly said, sliding an arm around the girl.

Jacey opened the album, and Rakmen stared at the ancient paneling on the opposite wall. "For dearest Kylie, because God needed you in heaven," Jacey read.

Rakmen wished she had a mute button.

"Why does God need a little girl?"

"I don't know," said Molly, all the ruin in her voice.

Rakmen had echoed Jacey's question every time some well-meaning neighbor had patted his mom on the shoulder and reminded her that *everything happens for a reason* or that *God has a plan*. Jacey turned the page, and a plump little boy with blue eyes stared out at them from a soft-focus Sears photo-center shot. The hand-lettered caption read *Our Guardian Angel*.

"I wanted a brother, not an angel," said Jacey. "It sucks being an only child." On the other side of her, Molly was rigid. Her sister had been her best friend. Jacey paused at another baby. Gold foil letters proclaimed She Watches Over Us from on High. "Why didn't my brother have one?"

The paneling on the opposite wall was brown. Near the floor there was water damage. Higher up, it was scuffed and dented. A stack of metal chairs tilted into the corner.

"Rakmen," Jacey demanded, pulling on his arm. "Why didn't Jordan have his own angel to keep him safe?"

"Angels are bullshit."

Jacey stared at the baby's picture. "Yeah . . ." she said, finally. "That's what I think too."

On the next page, a dark-skinned boy in a toddler-sized University of Oregon jersey clutched a football to his chest. "Is he their brother?" Jacey asked, nodding toward to the twins.

Molly nodded. "That's D'Shawn."

"What happened to him?"

"Cancer."

Jacey pointed to the dates under little boy's picture. "It's almost his birthday."

The pressure of the air around Rakmen changed. The mildewed basement choked him. Calendars were dangerous. Dora's birthday was a month away and then two weeks later, the anniversary of her death. They were coming for him.

Jacey pushed off the couch, taking the memory book with her.

"Coming to do some art?" Keri asked, flashing a too-wide smile.

The girl shook her head and went to stand beside D'Vareay, fidgeting until he looked up at her

"Whatchya want?"

"I don't know about the birthdays," she said.

D'Vareay squinted at her. "Huh?"

She opened the album in front of him. He dropped his gaze then tore it away in an instant. "What do you want?" he growled.

"I don't know what to do when it's my brother's birthday. What do you do for D'Shawn? Is there cake?"

"No cake."

D'Vareay and D'Mareay looked at each other, and Rakmen was sure there was an understanding between them, an agreement, a plan.

Trouble.

The art therapist tried to deflect Jacey. "You know, honey, the Jews light candles when someone dies."

Jacey considered this. "At the baby shower, we got this candle with numbers on it from one to twenty-one. You're supposed to light it on each birthday and let it burn down to the next number. Can I use that?"

"You mean . . . like . . . on your brother's birthday?" Keri seemed confused by the question.

"Yeah."

"But the candle's supposed to mark the child's age, right?"

Jacey nodded.

"Throw it away," Rakmen said. "They don't get to grow up."

31

"Don't be mean," said Molly. She patted the spot next to her on the couch. "Come here, Jacey. I'll tell you a story."

Rakmen checked his watch. He wanted out.

"When Rissa turned six and I was eight, there was a big storm on her birthday. She was afraid and climbed into bed with me. I ate a piece of chocolate and breathed on her with my chocolaty breath and she wasn't scared any more. So that's what we did every birthday after that."

"Chocolate breath?" Jacey asked.

"Yup."

"You were a good sister."

Molly tried to smile at her.

"What are you going to do now?" Jacey asked.

Molly shrugged. "Keep eating the chocolate, I guess."

"I really wanted to be a big sister," said Jacey, continuing to turn the pages of the memory book.

"I know you did."

Molly turned to a blank page of her sketch pad. Under her fingertips a nest of blankets took shape. A tangle of arms and hair and Rissa laughing in spite of the lightning crashing down.

Jacey tugged on Rakmen's arm. "I want to know something else."

Annoyance buzzed through him. Enough already with the questions that didn't have proper answers.

"Am I supposed to be working?"

He held up a hand to ward her off. "There are child labor laws. Now go away."

She shoved the open book in his face. Rakmen refused to look at the baby's picture. He did not need to know another one. She jabbed at the page. "It says, 'Her work on Earth is done.' She was a baby. And she was done?" Jacey's voice rose into a question.

Keri came up, wild-eyed. At least he wasn't the only one who didn't know what to do with Jacey.

"I'm ten," the girl announced, "and I haven't done anything."

At least Keri had the good sense to say nothing since she obviously didn't know what to say. Not like Rakmen's neighbor who'd said *I know how you feel; my dog died* or Great-Aunt Cecelia who'd reminded his mom that it was *for the best* as Dora would probably have been a sickly child.

It seemed to Rakmen that some people's work on Earth should be to shut the hell up.

"It doesn't mean crap," said Rakmen.

"How about this?" said Keri, finding her voice. "You can make a scrapbook page for Jordan next time you come. Bring a photo and I'll help you."

"I'm not sure I'll be back," said Jacey.

"Sure you will," said Keri.

Jacey ignored her and leaned into Rakmen. "Mom told Dad that she couldn't look at that empty crib another second and that she was leaving. I don't know what that means."

Leaving meant gone. It meant holes in everything. The walls and low ceiling pressed the air out of Rakmen. When the scraping of chairs upstairs signaled the end of the meeting, Rakmen shot out of the couch. Molly and the twins followed him upstairs.

Their moms were talking on the porch.

"Hi, guys," said his mom, stuffing a crumpled tissue into her pocket. Rakmen and the twins nodded at her.

Molly's mom slid an arm around her daughter's waist. "How was group?"

"You know. . . ." Molly shrugged. "It was group."

Why, Rakmen wondered, did they always need a status report from the basement? He didn't want to know what happened up here.

"So," said his mom, filling the empty space, "we're having a barbecue for Memorial Day. You're all invited. Four o'clock, okay? And bring a side dish or something."

A warm, damp hand slithered into his.

He couldn't get away from the little stalker.

"We'd love to come, wouldn't we, Jacey?" said Mrs. Tatlas.

Of course, they'd love to come. Just what Rakmen needed—

33

more face time with those two. He shook off Jacey's hand. "I'm going to the car."

"Be right there," said his mom, writing down their address for Molly's mom.

"Bye, Rakmen," Jacey yelled. He ignored her.

Mrs. Tatlas caught up with him at the car, and instantly his hackles rose. The last thing he needed was a lecture.

"I brought you some extra study materials for the final. Your grade will be okay if you learn this stuff." She handed Rakmen a stack of papers and gave him a thin smile, which made the jaggedness behind her eyes seem somehow more dangerous.

"Uh . . . thanks," Rakmen stammered.

"See you in class."

He nodded and watched Mrs. Tatlas tug Jacey down the sidewalk. The girl wasn't making it easy. She lagged behind, throwing glances at him over one shoulder. Her eyes begged him to call her back. He felt a rush of panic for the girl but shook it off.

Don't be stupid, he told himself. Her mom is fine. But as he buckled his seat belt, his unease grew. Sometimes there were cracks no one could see.

CHAPTER 5

After the last bell, Rakmen beelined for his locker. Juan was waiting for him, cap pulled low over his eyes and a basketball under one arm. "Let's go shoot hoops."

Every day, he asked.

Every day, Rakmen said no.

He couldn't remember the version of himself who loved the pebbled surface of the ball on his fingertips as he dribbled on the cracked courts in Pier Park.

"I've got to drop off some job applications on my way home," he said, "and then I have to study." Mrs. Tatlas's stack of notes was waiting.

Juan gave him a dirty look. "You don't have to be so perfect, you know."

"Perfect? That's a joke." He was the opposite of perfect—second-rate, defective, broken. "I just want to buy a car. That way I can take off when I want to."

"Come on, man. After the game my cousin will buy us beer."

Rakmen shook his head.

"Rakmen—" Juan was right in his face now. "You used to have fun. What's with all the goodie-two-shoes shit? Trying to impress that white girl you're lusting over?"

Heat raced up Rakmen's neck. His hands balled up at his sides. "Don't talk about her."

Juan laughed. "Oh, come on. You wanna tap that, and you know it." Before Rakmen knew what he was doing, his fists were up and Juan was backing off. "Take it easy. I'll lay off your girlfriend. No harm. No foul."

Rakmen dropped his fists, breathing hard.

"Good luck with the studying." Juan slipped into the crowded hall and disappeared.

Rakmen leaned against his locker and shut his eyes. Molly wasn't his girlfriend. Would never be his girlfriend. They weren't like other people. They never would be. Not as long as they met up in that musty basement once a month.

As he went back to loading his backpack, a sudden, sharp noise froze him in place. A thin, newborn cry. It was a sound that didn't belong in the halls at Roosevelt. Terror filled Rakmen. In one thudding heartbeat, he held Dora in his arms, smelled talcum powder, and felt the way she nestled against his chest. The baby cried again. The last thing he wanted was to see baby.

Or think baby.

Or know baby.

Yet the sound drew him to the door of Mrs. Tatlas's biology room.

Marissa stood, hip-cocked in low-rise jeans, holding her son. Through her sheer, tight shirt Rakmen could see the outline of a red bra. On the other side of the room, fleshy specimens floated in jars. Mrs. Tatlas's lips were compressed to a skeletal line. Like matching pits, the dark circles under her eyes sucked in light.

The baby cried again.

Marissa jiggled him and chomped her gum. "Little Tyrone was sick all week. That's why I missed class. Do I have any makeup stuff?" Wordlessly, Mrs. Tatlas handed her a packet. Marissa shifted the baby to her shoulder. Her gum made slobbery noises. "He didn't sleep last night. I'm so tired. You know how it is, since you're a mom and stuff."

Rakmen leaned forward, hands on his knees to try and calm the pitching in his stomach.

"Your son is very cute," said Mrs. Tatlas.

Oblivious to the sharp edges in her voice, Marissa giggled and cooed at the baby. "Yes, you are a cutie, cutie pie!"

"I'm late," said Mrs. Tatlas, grabbing her coat and bag. "Do the work. Take care of the baby." She barreled, blank-faced, past Rakmen, and he thought of what Jacey had said about her mom wanting to leave. She'd said that she was going away. He'd thought that meant moving or going on vacation, but the devastation spewing from Mrs. Tatlas made him wonder if she owned a gun.

He had a sudden flash of her fingers against cold metal, an ear-deafening blast, and the quickest way to get out of the dark. Rakmen followed Mrs. Tatlas out of the school, stunned by the realization that they had something in common. More than anything, they wanted out of Promise House, but they were so very stuck. As much as Mrs. Tatlas repulsed him, Rakmen was also drawn to her.

In the parking lot, she threw her bags into the trunk of the car and slammed it shut, but instead of driving away, she left the car and walked off campus.

He should leave.

Rakmen knew that, but he trailed her anyway. The street ended at a high bluff overlooking the river. She turned onto the walking trail, which paralleled the silvery water. Mrs. Tatlas moved quickly, her arms wrapped tightly around herself. She looked like a woman who would break all the plates in the house. She looked like she wished she could follow that river right out to the sea. Rakmen stopped walking and watched her go. Jacey was wrong about him being able to help. The best he could do was try and remember how things fall apart.

He sat on a bench overlooking the river and opened his notebook. He'd taken notes from the morning paper. *Abused and neglected Chihuahuas flood local animal shelters. Bomb scare at local high school. Girl, four, dies from E. coli poisoning.*

The surface of the river took on an oily sheen in the afternoon light. It ran deep and fast with the spring rain. Anything could be down there. On the next blank line in the notebook, he wrote *drowning, suicide, to the sea.*

He would stay out of the way.

He would get a job.

He would get a car.

And then he would get as far away from Promise House as he could.

• • •

After Starbucks and Safeway, Rakmen went to Ray's Auto Parts and Salvage, a shabby place with a peeling red and blue sign tucked around the corner from a second-run movie theater and a cavernous liquor store. Ray was his dad's best friend and the best shot he had at a summer job. Rakmen breathed in the smell of tires and metal.

And space.

No one here would bother him with feeling words. No one asking for skinny, extra-hot, super foamy macchiatos. Working here would be alright.

"Well, hey," said Ray, emerging from the crowded aisles of parts behind the counter. He was a short guy but muscled and wiry. His palms were perpetually etched in black grease from pulling parts out of junkers. "How's it?"

Rakmen shrugged.

"Your mom doing okay?"

"I think so."

Ray raised his eyebrows like he knew about the muffled fights Rakmen heard through the floor most nights.

"Anyway," said Rakmen, changing the subject, "I filled out the application you gave me. I'd really like to work here this summer."

"Can you pull parts?"

"Sure. Anything."

"Until the first time you get a big splat of oil in the face." Ray laughed. "Seriously though, wouldn't you rather go to basketball camp or Outward Bound or something?"

"What's that?" Rakmen asked, pulling the application out of his backpack.

"Hiking, camping, survival training. Real-life Man vs. Wild stuff."

"Like in the wilderness?"

"Exactly—all full of bears and cougars." Ray bared his teeth and pretended to claw at Rakmen. "And not the old lady kind."

Rakmen shook his head. "Not me. I wanna buy a car."

"That's my man," said Ray. "Then you'll be a paying customer." He slid Rakmen's job application under the counter. "I'm sure this'll work out, son. We'll have a good time."

Rakmen nodded. It was cool with Ray. You could be chill around him. Talk about cars and fishing and stuff. Ray wasn't always breathing down his neck. The bell at the front door rang as a customer came in. Time to go.

"Don't forget about the barbecue on Memorial Day," Rakmen said, as he headed for the exit. "Mom wants you to come early and keep Dad out of trouble."

"I'll be there," said Ray, "and don't worry about your mom and dad, kid. They'll get through this. You all will."

CHAPTER 6

On Memorial Day, Rakmen was in his mother's tamale assembly line with Juan, D'Vareay, D'Mareay, and Jacey. The girl dunked corn husks in a huge pot of water, pulling the yellow squares out with a flourish that sprayed water over the rest of them.

"Watch it," grunted D'Mareay as he rolled soft, pale dough into balls.

"Sorry," said Jacey and went back to submerging the tamale wrappers.

Juan took a dough ball from D'Mareay and patted it flat on the corn husk. "Is she coming?" Rakmen plunked down a spoonful of shredded pork in spicy, smoky chili sauce and ignored him. "Serious, man," said Juan, "I need to clamp eyes on the hotness. The way you clam up you must be all over her."

D'Vareay caught Rakmen's eye as they placed newly wrapped and tied tamales in the ever-growing pile of yellow rectangles. "She coming?"

"Yeah," Rakmen said, half-wishing Molly wouldn't be. This was other-side-of-the-tracks territory for her, and Juan was being an asshole. Rakmen smelled lighter fluid and heard a whoosh of flame from the backyard. Through the kitchen window he could see his dad, Ray, and Jacey's dad chatting over the now-roaring charcoal.

"I think Molly's super pretty," Jacey piped in, "except for that scar."

"Scar?" said Juan. "You didn't tell me she was messed up. Kinky."

"She got it when—" Jacey began, but Rakmen put a dough-covered hand over her mouth.

Jacey slapped away his hand and pummeled the tamale wrappers. It would be a miracle if she kept her mouth shut. Jacey moistened another corn husk and handed it to Juan, refusing to look at any of them.

"Keeping secrets doesn't make it go away," Jacey whispered.

"Out!" Rakmen roared, pointing through the back door.

Jacey shoved the pot, sending water slopping over the edge and across the counter. "I'm not helping you anymore."

She stomped out of the kitchen, and Rakmen mopped up the water with a towel, cursing.

"I see you already got a girlfriend," said Juan, thumbing at Jacey. "Guess that leaves Blondie for me."

"Leave it, man," said D'Vareay. "Molly's not for you."

Rakmen and D'Mareay tensed. They knew what D'Vareay meant, and they also knew that Juan would take it wrong.

Sure enough, he threw back his shoulders. "You don't think I'm good enough for her?"

"It's not that," said Rakmen.

Juan exhaled loudly, the expression on his face full of questions he wouldn't ask. *What happened to you, man? We were friends, weren't we?*

Rakmen looked away.

There was no point explaining. Promise House was wet concrete. It caught and held them, hardening around their limbs until they couldn't move.

"Good enough for who?" said Rakmen's mom, leading Molly and her mom through the house toward the backyard.

"For Mrs. Tatlas," Rakmen blurted. "Juan and I were talking about how hard her class is."

Molly raised an I-don't-believe-you eyebrow, but his mom went all boot-camp. "You will be good enough for her, *mijo. ¿Sí? ¿Sí?*"

For the moment, he didn't care about his plummeting grades.

What mattered was that Molly didn't think he was talking about her like she was a piece of ass. He liked her scar and her funny-sad sense of humor and even her sister, who he'd never get to meet. Juan was right. Rakmen was no player. But being with Molly made him feel like he wasn't up against a wall. Something more was possible.

"Do you need any help?" Molly asked.

Rakmen grinned at her and tied a strip of corn husk around the last tamale. "My work here is done," he said, wiping his hands on a towel. "Here you go, Mom."

"*¿Finito? Que bueno, mijo.*" His mom squeezed his arm. "You are free."

He led them outside where Jacey and the neighbor girl, Denise, were gyrating around the yard in hula hoops.

"Hi, Molly!" Jacey yelled. "We're having a contest!" In her excitement, she clipped Denise's hoop, sending it clattering to the ground. "I win! I'm the queen!"

"You cheated!" Denise hucked a dirt-covered Barbie at Jacey, whose hoop went flying.

"Barbie butt!"

"Dog nose!"

"Girls!" roared Jacey's dad, and Molly rushed over to help them work it out.

"Got any ear plugs?" Rakmen whispered to his dad, who winked at him and pulled two beers from the cooler, handing one to Ray and one to Jacey's dad.

"By all that is holy, I wish those two had volume control," he said, tipping back his beer.

Rakmen and the boys grabbed sodas and sat on the deck in the sun. Rakmen sat quietly nursing his Coke and trying to take stock. It was good to hear his dad talking about cars and the NBA draft. It was good to smell the lingering bite of lighter fluid over coals. Two more weeks, and he'd be done with school. One less thing for him to fail at. If he could get a job, earn some real money, there might be a way out after all.

An hour later, after the tamales had been steamed and the steaks charred, they were all crammed into the dining room around the regular table plus two more folding ones borrowed from a neighbor.

"Join hands," said his mother. Molly was across from Rakmen between Jacey and D'Vareay. "Come on, boys," his mom urged. With a groan, Rakmen reached toward Juan and D'Mareay. As far as he was concerned they were close enough already, but they clasped woodenly and bowed their heads.

"Dear Lord," his mother began, "we are so grateful to be together, to be fed, to be sheltered. Today, on Memorial Day, we remember those who have died so that we might sit around this table."

An ache rose in Rakmen's chest. The familiar, weighty feel of the dead enveloped him. His lungs grew leaden, but a chorus of amens broke through the dark edges at his vision. The boys beside him dropped hands like they were on fire.

The mothers began to pass plates of steaming tamales, extra bowls of chili sauce, platters of steak, and salad, and in the flurry, Rakmen began to breathe again. As he piled his plate, he caught Molly looking at him.

She gave him a sad smile and tucked her head so that a wave of hair hid her scar. He knew she'd felt them too, the dead ones. He scanned the faces around the table. They were a mashed-up, weird kind of almost-family. Just not the one he wanted.

"How's the job search going, Rakmen?" Jacey's dad asked.

He shrugged. "Cross your fingers I don't end up at Starbucks."

Molly laughed. "You'd make a cute barista."

"I've got some other options," said Rakmen, trying to catch Ray's eye.

His dad asked for the tamales. His mom passed the tray without looking at him. The twins' mom served her sons unwanted piles of salad, which they picked at. Jacey fidgeted with her spoon until her mother took it away.

"So Molly," his mom began, trying to fill in the empty spaces, "are you still playing soccer?"

Molly's forehead creased, puckering her scar. Soccer was before the accident. This was now. Her father answered for her. "Not this season. The sport's getting too rough. And we can't risk another concussion."

Methodically, Molly cut her steak in tiny bits.

She'd played defense, Rakmen knew, and she'd been good.

"How are things at the store?" his dad asked Ray.

"Fine. Can you pass the salt?"

A phone erupted into a series of chimes. The twins' mom checked her messages, shot dagger eyes at her sons, then stared again at the screen of her phone like it was a rattlesnake.

Silent alarm bells were going off all over. Rakmen elbowed D'Mareay. Molly nudged D'Vareay. The brothers grew instantly cagey. Their mother rose to her feet, quelling all talk at the table. The boys set down their utensils and braced for it.

"Boys!" she boomed, holding out the phone. "What in God's name is this?" Every eye in the room was fixed on the screen as the boys' mom set it in the middle of the table with dangerous precision. Like the insistent gravity of a black hole, it tugged them forward. Rakmen rose so he could look down at the screen.

The picture of the Alberta Street overpass on Interstate 5 had been snapped from a moving car. He could see the edge of the windshield in the corner of the frame. The concrete wall of the overpass filled the rest of the phone. Every inch was a riot of Technicolor spray paint—a birthday message to D'Shawn.

Rakmen recognized the boys' signature style instantly.

"It's beautiful," said Molly. Both boys flashed her a rare grin.

"Shut up," their mom snapped. She grabbed D'Vareay, who had the bad luck to be closest, and hoisted him out of his seat. Then she proceeded to nab D'Mareay. "Say thank you for dinner," she commanded, retrieving the phone.

"Thanks," they mumbled.

Rakmen half expected her to clap the boys in cuffs, and he stifled the urge to tell them to run for it.

"Tricia," said Rakmen's mom, "don't leave."

She turned stiffly in the doorway. "We really appreciate being included, but I really must take my hoodlums home."

"I know that's bad behavior..." His mom faltered underneath a withering glare. "Really bad, but it's good that they're expressing themselves. Grieving people need to talk." Rakmen's mom shot a pointed look at his dad, who rose and left the table without a word.

Tricia propelled the boys through the front door. It slammed shut behind them and broke the hush in the room. Suddenly everyone was in a hurry to go.

"Come on, Molly," said her mom, bustling toward the door.

Mrs. Tatlas pulled Jacey out of her chair. "Us too, sweetie."

"I'm not done!" the girl wailed. Her dad picked her up and headed for the front hall. Rakmen's mom trailed them out, stammering assurances that they didn't have to leave. Everyone said *good-bye* and *thanks* and *wasn't this nice* and *see you again soon*. They said the things they were supposed to say.

Rakmen caught up with Ray as he was shrugging into his coat. "Hey, school's out in two weeks."

"Yeah? Good. You must be psyched."

"I'll be ready to go to work right away. I don't need any time off or anything."

Ray avoided his eyes. "About that . . ."

Rakmen shoved his hands into his pockets and wrapped the tattered notebook in a stranglehold. This morning, he'd scribbled headlines. *Contaminated mud from Willamette River superfund site shifting into main channel. Unexploded WWII ordnance unearthed by children in McMinnville.* "Look, man, I'm sorry," said Ray, rubbing his temples. "Things aren't so good at the store."

Rakmen's limbs felt impossibly heavy. "But you said it was fine. The junkyard is always busy."

His mom came up beside them. "What's going on, Ray?"

"One of my guys at the junkyard got hurt on the job. He's got some ambulance chaser suing me."

"But I need that job," said Rakmen, more loudly than he meant to. Jacey's family stopped halfway out of the door.

Ray held up his hands and shrugged. "I know it sucks. I'm sorry, but I can't afford to hire you."

Rakmen pressed his fists against his thighs to keep them from bashing holes in the walls.

"Thanks for dinner, Mercedes," said Ray before escaping past the Tatlases. The family congealed around Jacey, who was having some kind of shoe malfunction.

His mother turned from the door, looking stunned. "What are you going to do all summer?"

"I don't know," said Rakmen, his voice acid. "Sit around and listen to you and Dad fight, I guess."

"Rakmen—" his mom warned.

"Assuming you ever stay in the same room together for longer than two seconds."

Her whole body tensed, and her face went rigid. When she finally spoke, her voice was low and pinched like the words were extracted against her will. "This isn't about your dad and me. You need to stay out of trouble."

"Well, I can't!" he snarled, throwing up his arms. She flinched, and he knew that he was an asshole. The sick feeling in his gut rose into his throat. "Look—" he said, flat and cold. "There's no point trying to make things like they were."

They stared at each other. Different planets a million miles apart.

"Hey, you two," said Mrs. Tatlas, putting a hand on his mom's arm. "It's not my business, I know, but can I throw a crazy idea out there?"

Rakmen and his mom broke their stare-down.

"Sure, Leah," said his mom, regaining her composure. "He probably needs summer school, right?"

Rakmen's eyes narrowed.

His teacher shook her head. "He did okay on that last assignment. If he keeps it up, he'll be fine." The tension in his mother eased a sliver. "So here's the deal. I need a change of scenery." Rakmen's hackles rose, remembering what Jacey had said about her mom wanting to take off. "Jacey and I are going to spend July and August up at my Uncle Leroy's cabin in Canada. It's on a lake in the woods. It'll be nice."

La-ti-da for you, thought Rakmen. Suddenly, Jacey was pressing against his side like a dog wanting its head scratched. He stepped away, but she glommed on, sliding her hand into his.

"That sounds nice for you, Leah." His mom wasn't doing a very good job of keeping irritation out of her voice.

"I bring it up," Mrs. Tatlas continued, looking a little embarrassed, "because Jacey's being a bit stubborn." Rakmen shook his hand free of Jacey's grasp. "She doesn't want to go—"

Jacey wrapped her arms around herself, hunching over so she seemed even smaller than usual. Of course she didn't want to go, and for the same reason that he really needed that job with Ray. Neither wanted to spend the summer with mothers like theirs.

"I don't understand what you're telling me, Leah," said his mom, sounding way beyond tired.

"Jacey wants Rakmen to go with us."

He jerked to his full height.

"What?" his mom asked.

"George can't get the time off," said Mrs. Tatlas, gesturing to her husband, who was halfway out the door and clearly wanted to get all the way out. "Jacey's got it in her head that Rakmen's her own personal Superman or something." She laughed nervously. "It's a little weird, but we'd love to have him, especially since he's got the time now."

"Someone's got to take care of me," Jacey muttered.

A mask fell over Mrs. Tatlas's face, turning her features corpse-like.

"Jacey. Out. Now," said her dad.

The girl skittered past her mother and down the front steps.

"Thanks for the offer, Leah. We'll think about it," said his mom.

Rakmen swallowed back his rising nausea.

The thinking was done. A cabin in the woods with the two of them wasn't a vacation; it was a prison sentence, and besides, he couldn't be trusted to take care of anyone.

CHAPTER 7

After helping his mom clean up, Rakmen retreated to his room and flopped on the bed. The fading smell of charcoal from the grill curled up from the backyard, and the party at the neighbor's was still going strong. He wanted to sleep, but it was only a few weeks from the longest day of the year and still light outside. Besides, a tight ball of unease rattled inside his ribcage.

His dad had not come home.

A few days ago, while thumbing through one of his mom's books on surviving the loss of a child, he'd come up with a statistic, which he'd carefully penciled into the notebook. *In the majority of cases, the marriage does not survive the loss.*

And the walls in this house were thin. Overhearing was something Rakmen couldn't escape. His dad wanted space. He wanted to be left alone. His mom wanted to talk and talk and talk as if words alone could bring back babies.

He opened the notebook and wrote *'Til death do us part.*

He crumpled the book in one hand, straining to tell if the rumbling engine noise outside was his dad's truck or the neighbor's. A minute later he heard the front door open and close. He waited for his mother to speak. She was there. He'd left her on the couch, re-reading that book, the one about grief.

Instead, the TV blared SportsCenter. The familiar buzz of the broadcast filled him with relief. He pushed off the bed. He could catch the game with Dad and forget about how Memorial Day had gone down in flames, but as he opened the door, the TV voice cut off mid-sentence.

"I was watching that," said his dad.

Rakmen froze with his hand on the doorknob.

"You can't keep pretending that nothing has happened," said his mom.

"That's not what I'm doing." His dad's voice was gravelly and tired. Rakmen crept to the top of the stairs, drawn unwillingly to watch the coming disaster.

His mother was shrill. "You won't talk or go to therapy, so what are you doing?"

"There's nothing to do, Mercedes. She died. Talking doesn't change that."

Rakmen could fill every line of every page in his notebook with *she died, she died, she died*, and it would never be enough.

She died in my arms.

He edged down the stairs like a guilty man to the gallows.

"If you don't talk about it, how do you expect our son to work through this?"

They should know everything that happened the night Dora died. He felt like he might explode with it.

"Rakmen's fine," his dad growled as Rakmen reached the bottom of the stairs.

"Fine? He's about as far from fine as you can get. He's almost flunking out of school. He's depressed. He's volatile. You'd know if you paid any attention at all to your kids—"

"Kids?"

From the shadow of the hall, Rakmen could see the dangerous currents swirling on his father's face.

His mother took a step back. "You know what I meant."

49

"Yeah, I do," said his father. "You mean it's my fault she's dead."

Rakmen wanted to scream *it was me* but the words stuck in his throat.

"I didn't say that. But—"

"But what?!" his dad said, each word an attack.

Tears poured down his mother's face. "You're the nurse," she shouted. "You should've known something was wrong."

Over her head, Rakmen could see Dora's picture on the mantel. Her dark eyes pierced his body. And suddenly he was running. Out the front door, down the steps. He slammed his feet into the sidewalk and pumped his arms until he was an engine, incapable of feeling anything but the urge to go and never come back. He half-slid around the corner, darting through traffic, sprinting past pedestrians. Running trumped thinking and memory and all the things that kept him up at night.

Rakmen ran until he was a few blocks from Pier Park. His lungs screamed for air and explosions of black dotted his peripheral vision. Sweat dripped into his stinging eyes. He swiped at it with his sleeve, ducked into the shade of the huge firs on either side of the bike path, and collapsed on an empty bench.

The energy that had propelled him drained away until Rakmen was empty, an old tin can, worthless for anything but target practice. It shouldn't have been Dora. It should have been him. Then his parents would have held joy between them instead of the hollow space that was Rakmen.

Minutes passed. Rakmen's breath slowed and his pulse returned to normal. The steady thump of dribbled basketballs came from the courts up a set of stairs to his left. There were birds chittering up high. A splinter from the rough wooden bench jabbed him in the back of the thigh. He couldn't move to save his life.

He couldn't go home.

He had no job.

No family.

Stuck. He was always stuck.

Rakmen scuffed the toe of his sneaker in the gravel below the bench and watched an old Hispanic guy in a Parks Department uniform empty the trash can at the base of the stairs. That'd be him in fifty years, hauling bags of other people's castoffs. Rakmen closed his eyes and dropped his head to his chest.

A second later, an ear-splitting screech of wood against metal jolted him to his feet. The groundskeeper was still bent over the trash can, but a skateboarder had jumped the stair rail and was skidding down in a blur.

The old man dove out of the way, the metal trash can lid went flying, and the boarder skidded to a stop.

Rakmen took the stairs two at a time and knelt beside the groundskeeper. "Are you alright?"

"*Dios mío, que gabacho loco,*" he said as Rakmen helped him up.

The skater, a gaunt-faced white guy in his twenties, flipped up his board and pulled his knit cap nearly down to his eyes. "Man, I nailed that. You okay?"

Rakmen wanted to rip his face off.

"Young man," said the groundskeeper, brushing dirt and pine needles off his coveralls, "There is a skate park over there." He pointed through the trees in the direction of the baseball diamonds. "These rails are off-limits."

"Off-limits for who?" sneered the skater, lighting a cigarette. "Sneak back over the border, old man. I'll skate where I like."

Roaring filled Rakmen's ears, obliterating the sounds from the basketball court and the distant hum of traffic. An outsized savagery bloomed in his belly and raged through his limbs. Face first. Arms second. He lurched forward, fists clenched.

The groundskeeper tried to stop him, but Rakmen swung hard from underneath and took the skater in the jaw. The impact ricocheted up his arm, the man's chin rocketed back, and the cigarette whirligigged in the air.

Specks of saliva clung to the corners of the skater's crooked lips. Surprise, then anger, then disgust flashed through his eyes as if he was above fighting someone so worthless. Rakmen's fists curled again. He wanted to erase that sneer. He threw a wild punch, but this time the skater was ready. He swung his board up hard, connecting with the side of Rakmen's head and throwing him off-balance.

Through the reverberations in his skull, Rakmen heard a guttural roar coming from somewhere, his own throat maybe. He lurched forward, plowing his head into the skater's stomach. Together they crashed to the ground. For a split second, they were chest-to-chest, too close and strangely intimate. Then the skater was digging his hands into the sides of Rakmen's face, scraping flesh, inching toward his eyes.

He pushed Rakmen's head back to the splintering point. Fire shot down his spine. With a fierce jerk, Rakmen broke free of the skater's grasp and pounded his head into the man's chest. Under him, the skater thrashed and bucked, wrenching loose with a vicious jab to Rakmen's kidney.

He flipped Rakmen onto his back and scrambled to his feet. Rakmen was trying to stand with the singular goal of wrapping his hands around that asshole's neck when the skater kicked him hard in the side. The sound was a pumpkin dropped on asphalt. The pain was a black flood. The skater kicked him again, and Rakmen crumpled.

"You're nothing," the skater jeered through bloody teeth.

Rakmen couldn't be sure if the words came from that gash of a mouth or from those puncture wound eyes, but they reverberated through him as he passed out.

Nothing.

Nothing.

Nothing.

CHAPTER 8

The old man was calling 911 when Rakmen regained consciousness.

"Don't," Rakmen said, his tongue thick in his mouth. He'd thrown the first punch. Cops would never side with him.

"You're hurt."

Rakmen tried to shake his head. His brain seemed to bang against the side of his skull with every movement. He held his head steady, looking at the still-spinning trees overhead, and reached for the man's arm. "Please. No."

Squatting on his haunches, the old man gazed at him a long time.

Rakmen willed himself to pass out again. Instead his body resumed. The world stilled. His breath returned to slow and steady. Everything ached, throbbed, stabbed.

The groundskeeper pursed his lips and frowned at Rakmen. "Can you stand?"

Rakmen stood, shrugged off the old man's arm, and began to drag himself home. The blocks he'd sprinted stretched out before him. It was all concrete and pain and returning to worse than a beating.

He could hear his parents fighting as he went up the front steps.

He walked right in. At least they'd have something new to yell about.

His mother had cried, screamed at him, and then cried again, a good show of full-on parental shit fit. But really, she had been crying for Dora. Rakmen's father had cleaned his son's wounds in silence, diagnosed a broken rib without sympathy, and prescribed a double dose of ibuprofen. Rakmen was some patient on his rounds. A stranger.

Rakmen had been banished to his room. No one checked in before bed. No one woke him for school the next day. Now it was nearly five o'clock. He'd stayed in bed all day, propped up on pillows to protect the worst of his bruises, and trying not to think about anything. His phone hadn't rung once.

When he heard his parents come home from work, Rakmen turned away from the door, even though resting on that side made the egg-sized lump on his head throb like a battering ram inside his skull. He breathed in shallow gasps. Inhaling too deeply sent pain stabbing through a rib on his left side.

There was a knock on his door. He ignored it, but the door opened anyway. Rakmen pretended to sleep. The desk chair scraped against the floor. He could hear the weight of his father settling into it. The mattress shifted as his mom sat beside him, sending a redoubled round of aches through his body.

"We need to talk," she said.

Rakmen rolled over, blinking at her through swollen, slitted eyes.

His dad sat in the desk chair, elbows on thighs, his head resting on the tips of his fingers. "What's your pain level?" he asked, without looking up.

"What am I? One of your patients?" Rakmen said. His dad's lips pinched into a tight line, but he didn't respond. "I get it," Rakmen continued. "I'm such a big disappointment to you that you won't even look at me." He pushed himself to a sitting position, ignoring the screams of his injuries, welcoming the stab in his chest. Level eight. It was what he deserved.

"This isn't about you," said his mom.

"That guy totally had it coming to him. Complete jerk-off." Now his mom wasn't looking at him either. She stared at her hands, limp in her lap. Rakmen sensed that he might have misread the stakes of the situation. Badly.

"So I'm grounded, right? For like the rest of my life. Fine." His dad cleared his throat, but Rakmen cut him off. "I'm sorry, okay? I shouldn't have gotten in a fight." His mom started to cry. The space between his dad in the chair and his mom on the bed seemed vast and unbridgeable. He knew, suddenly, that they weren't here to talk about the fight.

His dad cleared his throat again. "What we're trying to say is that things aren't going very well for us."

Rakmen tried to disappear into the rumbling sounds of the evening commute outside. Desperation settled over the room like poison gas. Since Dora died, they'd faked everything. A united front. Stiff upper lips. Acting normal. Barbecues. They'd tiptoed around like everyone was made of glass. The fatal mistake was expecting things to get better.

His mother wiped away her tears and spoke to her hands. "Your dad and I have processed your sister's passing in very different ways."

"So that's it?" Rakmen said. "You're getting divorced without even trying?"

His mom's head snapped up. "I didn't say divorce."

"But that's what you are saying, isn't it? Enough with the therapy talk."

"You will stop, son," said his dad, finally meeting his eyes. "Stop with the drama like this is all about you. We're not getting divorced—"

The *yet* dangled in the air between them.

"But we do need some time to refocus our marriage," his mom finished.

Rakmen imagined that he could hear the shattering of glass as things fell apart. Death. Divorce. They were fighting words, permanent words. And he was mad again, ready to punch someone in the face even if it meant getting the shit kicked out of him again. He spread his arms toward his parents in a gesture that said be my guest. They could knock themselves out trying to fix what was broken.

"Right now," said his dad, "we're very focused on you, your grades, and now this." He gestured at Rakmen's black eyes. "Fighting. You don't have a job lined up or any activities this summer. It's not a recipe for success."

"I'm not a cake mix," Rakmen muttered.

"We need some space to work on our issues," said his mom, "and we think you need a change of scene. Away from the memories."

Rakmen was rocking back and forth in the bed the way he'd been rocking Dora to sleep the night she died. He hadn't noticed her breathing change until it was too late. And then there was screaming and his dad wrenching her from his arms and the way he could remember the pattern on the rug in that room exactly.

"You're sending me away," he said.

"It's a great opportunity for new experiences." The false cheer in his mom's voice slid down his spine like ice water. "Leah said she spent all her summers at the lake cabin when she was a kid and loved it."

Of course, they were sending him away. He was the left-behind reminder of what they had lost. They would be better off without him.

"You can swim and fish," his dad added.

"I don't know how to fish," said Rakmen, then the exact meaning of what they were saying fell into place and he nearly choked. "You want me to go with Mrs. Tatlas and her psycho daughter to the middle of freaking nowhere? Are you crazy? I'm not doing that."

His mom began to explain, but his dad cut her off. "This is not a choice."

Rakmen swung his head from one to the other and back again, trying to read their faces. He knew they were desperate, but he'd had no idea they were so far gone. Mrs. Tatlas wasn't a life raft. She was a sinking ship.

"You can't do this," he protested. "She's not right in the head. You've seen her. She's worse than you guys—"

His mom stiffened. "She is grieving. There's nothing wrong with that. And she's been good to you. Extra help on that last test and now this offer to take you on vacation."

"Vacation?" Mrs. Tatlas was half in this world and half in the grave. His mom couldn't see it, and his dad didn't seem to care. Fear slid through Rakmen. Nothing good could come from following her. "Please, Dad" he said, imploring. "I won't get in the way. I won't fight again. I'll find a job."

A tired, sad smile rolled across his dad's face and then faded. He reached over and squeezed Rakmen's shoulder. "This family has been through a lot. I'll do what I have to do here. You might be surprised what you get out of the summer if you're open to it. It's time to man up. For both of us."

CHAPTER 9

Molly leaned into Rakmen's shoulder. "I can't believe they're sending you away."

"Me neither." It was the last day of June, and the two of them sat on the porch steps leaning against his dad's old army duffel, waiting.

"Promise House is going to suck without you," she said.

"It sucked with me."

Molly laughed. "You're right. It did."

He shifted against some unidentified lump in the duffel. Bear mace? Snake bite kit? Who knew what Mom had packed in anticipation of his two-month sentence to the wilderness. She'd gone off her rocker at the army surplus store buying boots, rain gear, bug repellent, a flashlight, and even a sheath knife that looked more gang-banger than Boy Scout.

"This is gonna be worse," he said.

"There's nothing worse."

"Jacey," Rakmen offered, raising one eyebrow.

Molly elbowed him. "She's not that bad."

Rakmen snorted. Jacey had called three times this morning to remind him to eat dinner early because they had to leave for the airport at six o'clock sharp. "You could be wrong," Molly continued.

"You're staying on a lake. Maybe you can learn to water ski."

"I'll probably break my neck."

"That's cheery."

He kept the lid on his real worry—Mrs. Tatlas. He doubted she could keep it together long enough to do anything as complicated as water skiing. She could do far worse than break plates, and he'd be a long way from anyone who could help. "Anyway," he said, nudging Molly's forearm and staring at the sprinkling of freckles there. "You didn't have to come for the send-off. Couldn't wait to get rid of me, huh?"

She snorted. "There's your girlfriend."

The Tatlases' battered blue Subaru wheezed around the corner. Jacey hung out the window waving so hard he thought her arm might fall off.

"I can't believe this," said Rakmen.

"Hey, before they get out, I want to give you something." Molly handed him a small wrapped box.

"What? You didn't have to do that."

"I thought it would be nice if you came back."

Rakmen tore through the paper to find a Garmin GPS. "Wow! Thanks. This is amazing." He couldn't imagine ever affording something so nice. And his hand was very close to Molly's on the box.

"Promise you won't get lost?" Her fingers slid closer. Warmth rushed through him, an unfamiliar lightness. She knew him and understood him and still wanted to graze his fingertips with her own.

And he was about to fly nearly three thousand miles away from her.

Still, Rakmen grinned. If Molly Campbell didn't want him lost, he was definitely NOT getting lost.

Jacey bounded, rabbit-like, toward them, jittering to a stop inches from his knees. "What's that? Can I see it? What's it do?" She squeezed in between them and wheedled it out of his hands, squealing.

Save me, he mouthed over the girl's rumpled head, but Molly only smiled and shrugged. Jacey's parents joined them, her dad awkwardly shaking Rakmen's hand and Mrs. Tatlas looking like the effort of standing was almost too much. Rakmen could see red rimming her

59

eyes. The heaviness flooded back in, dousing the spark that had passed between his fingers and Molly's. He was condemned.

"I've got something for you too, kiddo," Molly said, taking the GPS out of Jacey's hands and handing it back to Rakmen. She reached into her purse and gave Jacey a small box wrapped in yellow tissue paper. "Here you go."

Jacey tore off the wrapping. "Wow, wow, wow!" she shrieked, flinging her body into Molly's arms. "You're the best!" She rushed to her parents to show off the pink digital camera. "Can you believe this?"

"Oh, Molly," Mrs. Tatlas said. "We really can't . . ."

"I wanted to," said Molly, standing to hug Mrs. Tatlas. She squeezed Jacey's arm again. "Rakmen will teach you how to use it."

Behind them, the screen door opened, and Rakmen's and Molly's parents came out for the big goodbye. Rakmen wished everyone wasn't making such a big show of it.

"It's time to go," said Mr. Tatlas. "Can I give you a hand with that, Rakmen?"

Jacey wrapped her arms around his duffel. "I got it!" When she'd hefted it a foot off the ground, her whole body began to wobble.

"You're gonna kill yourself," Rakmen said, scooping it out of her arms before she toppled.

The three mothers froze, and Rakmen felt the chill that followed the word he couldn't call back. For several moments, there was too much silence and too much space. When the women forced themselves back into motion, each one looked at her empty hands as if she could weigh absence. Together, they walked to the car like mourners. Only Jacey jigged and bopped like she was going to a party.

Rakmen breathed in the summer evening—the bite of diesel in the air, garden dirt, and burgers cooking next door. This was what he knew, but it no longer felt like home. He was a runaway truck with burned out brakes. The ache that filled Rakmen pulsed in his bones, white-cold and penetratingly deep. With leaden arms, he hoisted his duffel into the trunk. Dad swept him into a bear hug, slapping his back so hard it sent a jolt of pain through his healing rib. Molly was next in line. She whispered, "Come back safe," and her lips grazed his ear. He thought of the moth against the bars and wanted to crush her to his chest.

Jacey pulled him into the backseat, and the smile on her face was so wide you could drive a semi through it. His mom leaned in to kiss him one more time. "I'll miss you, *mi corazón.*"

Another fragile thing in a cage of bone. *Mi corazón*, my heart.

That was the place he didn't want to go.

Dora's heart-shaped face, every detail of her tiny lips and silky eyelashes. The way he'd noticed everything but her overworked heart grinding to a halt.

The car's engine whined to life.

He choked out his last good-byes.

And before he knew it, Rakmen was skimming through his city as if he didn't belong there. Beside him, Jacey snapped pictures with her new camera—Juan's favorite taqueria, a bedraggled Chinese New Year dragon rotting in a parking lot, the bridge that reminded him of church windows.

CHAPTER 10

Rakmen slept for most of the flight from Portland to Chicago, waking only once when Jacey spilled ginger ale in her lap. Mrs. Tatlas mopped up the mess in strained silence. The girl's apology spilled out after the mess—*I'msorryI'msorryI'msorry*. When her mother didn't respond, Jacey curled up, stuck a piece of hair into her mouth, and buried her face against Rakmen's shoulder.

They slept until the plane thudded down the runway. Rakmen's sleeve was damp where she had pressed against it, but he didn't know if the wet was sweat or drool or tears. It was dark in Chicago, the middle of the night. Rain streaked the windows. They dragged themselves off the plane and into the terminal to wait for the next flight.

Their gate was near a security checkpoint. A TSA agent with a wispy mustache and a paunch that strained against his uniform swabbed hands for bomb residue. Another, an older woman with a bad dye job, stared into the luggage scanning screen, the contents of each carry-on revealed in X-ray black and white.

Rakmen flattened his notebook against his thigh.

September 11th. Homemade explosives. Planes going down.

He'd been little when the towers fell, had grown up in a world where they could.

Nauseous and unsettled from the time change and sour airport smells, Rakmen shifted in the uncomfortable plastic seat, watching Mrs. Tatlas out of the corner of one eye. She felt dangerous. He didn't want to get on the airplane with her.

The security line had thinned, finished. The TSA agents were talking. He couldn't help overhearing. The woman had a husband with cancer. The fat guy said his mom did too, and he knew he should stop smoking, but he couldn't. It was the only pleasure he had.

D'Shawn hadn't smoked. No one in his family had. But cancer snuck in, waiting for an opportunity, quiescent until it exploded. *Civilian casualties. Hidden threats. Security breaches.*

As soon as they boarded the flight from Chicago to Toronto, Rakmen balled up his jacket and tried to sleep against the window, but when a family with a sleepy toddler and a baby sat across the aisle from them, Mrs. Tatlas nudged him awake. "Switch with me." He blinked at her, blurry with exhaustion. "Take the aisle."

The baby squawked as the dad tried to settle him against his chest.

Mrs. Tatlas winced. "Please," she said through gritted teeth.

They snarled the procession of embarking passengers as he, Jacey, and Mrs. Tatlas switched places. She plastered her face to the window, staring out into the dark nothing and the rain.

The baby cried all the way to Toronto. "It's okay, baby. It's okay. Everything is okay," the baby's father whispered ceaselessly.

There were men who put bombs in bags at the finish line of marathons.

People lost their legs.

●　●　●

In the thin light of dawn, they were in a rental car heading north. Mrs. Tatlas, hunched over the wheel, hit scan on the stereo. The radio flicked past Christian stations and French stations and classical music and talk shows about fishing. She settled on *'80s* rock.

Next to him in the backseat of the moving vehicle, Jacey took pictures of the roller coaster at Canada's Wonderland, a captive herd of buffalo, and fields of corn.

"They won't come out," he told her.

"They will."

"They'll be blurry."

"But the good kind. The blurry that says go fast!" She bounced in the seat, pointing her camera at him. He held his hands up in front of his face, but she took his picture anyway.

An hour outside of the city, they stopped for coffee and donuts at Tim Hortons. Bright signs inside proclaimed that he could donate and help the Children's Foundation send a child to camp. The posters had pictures of all kinds of kids—black, white, Asian, Indian—grinning ear to ear as they navigated a ropes course.

Mrs. Tatlas had promised the summer would be something like that, all sun sparkly and wholesome, but she hardly looked like a camp counselor. Her clothes were wrinkled from sleeping in them all night. The lines of her face were thin cracks, spreading out from her eyes, rumpling around her lips.

"I'll have a chocolate chip cookie," said Jacey.

"It's breakfast time." Mrs. Tatlas's voice was a low monotone. "Have a donut."

Jacey peered up her. "That makes no sense. How's a donut different from a cookie?"

Her mom inhaled slowly, nostrils flaring.

Through his own exhaustion, Rakmen could still hear that baby on the plane crying. Sending the kids to camp was not beginning well. He stepped between the two of them and put his arm on Jacey's shoulder. "Let's get Canadian maple."

She squinted at him. "Is it chocolate?"

He shook his head. "Nope. Pudding in the middle, though. It's still dessert for breakfast."

"Okay."

Mrs. Tatlas handed him a Canadian twenty-dollar bill. "Coffee."

He ordered two Canadian maples, two milks, and a trucker-sized coffee.

Back on the road again, they kept driving north.

Farmland gave way to rougher terrain. Whether it was the coffee or something else, Mrs. Tatlas seemed to perk up. She sat a little taller and began pointing out things, nature stuff and biology. The jagged rocks jutting up on either side of the road were granite. The Day-Glo stuff splattered all over them was lichen—half fungus, half algae. The bright orange and yellow made Rakmen think of D'Mareay and D'Vareay and their many cans of spray paint.

"Are we gonna see a bear?" Jacey asked, as she took way too many pictures of a huge, domed rock covered with ferns.

"Maybe," said Mrs. Tatlas, like that would be a good thing.

"Maybe?" Rakmen repeated. No one had said anything about bears when they roped him into this sorry excuse for a summer. Oh right, this wasn't supposed to be fun.

"Probably not, though," Mrs. Tatlas continued. "In all the time I've spent up here, I've only seen a bear once." Rakmen leaned his head against the backseat and stared at the ceiling. Every cell in his body wanted to get out of the car.

"What about moose?" Jacey asked, as they passed yet another roadside campground with a picture of a moose on the sign.

"Good chance of that."

On second thought, he might be better off in the car. No moose. No bears. Only Jacey, bouncing in her seat like a jack-in-the-box.

After nearly four hours on the road, they stopped for groceries in what Mrs. Tatlas said was the last town before the lake and cabin. For the rest of the trip, Rakmen was smashed in between a gigantic package of toilet paper, brown paper bags full of canned beans, a five-pound bag of rice, hunks of cheddar cheese, a basket of peaches, and ominously, a dozen mouse traps.

"This is it." Mrs. Tatlas slowed the car onto the shoulder and pointed to a narrow, gravel road diving into the trees. If you could call it a road. It looked like no one had driven down it in ages.

"Are you sure?" Jacey asked.

Rakmen took in the high grass in the median of the track and the eroded gullies on either side. "Uh . . . are we in like Siberia or something? Where are the people?"

"This doesn't look like a real road," said Jacey.

Mrs. Tatlas redoubled her grip on the wheel and turned into the dark tunnel of trees. "It's a driveway." There were also potholes large enough to lose a cat in. Rakmen shifted nervously in the cramped backseat. Branches scraped and hissed against the side of the car as they bounced over the rutted road. Molly's vision of him water skiing with the happy camp kids was evaporating. The trees were so dense, and so many branches crisscrossed every available inch of space, that he could hardly believe there was a lake in there at all.

"Mom! Can we swim right away?" asked Jacey, pulling off her shoes and socks in preparation.

Rakmen stared at her as she scanned left and right to catch the first glimpse of their destination. The girl really was bats, but there was something contagious in her eagerness, and Rakmen found himself searching the trees for some twinkle of sun on water.

They'd taken Dora to Sauvie Island when she was ten days old. He sat with her in the backseat as Dad drove out Reeder Road toward the beaches on the Columbia River—not the nude beaches, the regular ones. Her newborn clothes were still too big for her and when she opened her mouth to squawk, he'd let her suck on his finger. And for some reason, even though everything else was ruined, that memory still made him happy.

The front tire hit a ridge of rock, and the car lurched forward suddenly. Rakmen flung out his arms to keep the grocery bags from sliding to the floor. Mrs. Tatlas swerved around another rock, made a sharp turn to the right, and stopped with a squeal in front of a low wall of broken cinderblocks.

She shut off the engine. "Well, we made it."

They piled out of the car and stretched.

Directly in front of Rakmen, a square building with weathered, gray shingles squatted on the edge of Vesper Lake. Shrouded in the shade of six huge trees, the cabin looked like it was waiting for someone to sit on it. Nothing twinkled. Not the dust-coated windows of the cabin, not the layer of pine needles on the ground, and definitely not the greenish surface of the lake.

Ignoring everything, Jacey careened toward the water. The soft plumping sound of her feet gave way to a splash and a squelch. She stopped knee deep, yelling at the top of her lungs. "Gross! It stinks! Mom, I'm sinking!"

Rakmen followed Mrs. Tatlas to the edge of the water, where Jacey was indeed sinking in black, oily muck. Farting sounds and the companion stench rose around her in a ring of bubbles. A few feet beyond there was probably water, but it was so choked and clotted with plants that Rakmen couldn't be sure. Mrs. Tatlas took Jacey's hand and helped her pull free from the muck with a stinky, sucking pop. Out in the lily pads, a frog began croaking like a bullhorn, and a red-headed bird swooped past them, chattering like machine-gun fire. Jacey scowled down at her muddy legs.

"Where's the lake?" she demanded.

Mrs. Tatlas's shoulders rose and fell with a big, worn-out sigh. She gestured toward the water. "Out there, beyond the bay."

Rakmen couldn't see anything lake-ish. No place to swim. No place to stretch his limbs and pull against the water. The momentary buoyancy when he'd remembered the day at the river collapsed. He'd done it again—expected something better—and again, he got slapped down and knocked out.

This was no happy kids' camp. This wasn't a fresh start. This was what he had to carry for the rest of his life. There was no better ahead.

"You told me it was a lake," Jacey whined. "You know, water? This is a swamp."

Mrs. Tatlas grimaced and headed for the cabin.

Jacey's lower lip was trembling. "Look at me. I'm disgusting."

He forced a smile and tried to joke with her. "Want me to take your picture, swamp monster?"

"It's not funny," she whimpered. "This sucks."

"I know," he said, taking her hand and pulling her toward the car. "Let's get you cleaned up."

They sat on the retaining wall, and Jacey swabbed her legs with a wad of Kleenex while Rakmen watched Mrs. Tatlas wrestle with the lock on the cabin. When she forced the door open, clouds of dust billowed out of the crooked door frame. Mrs. Tatlas went inside and immediately started coughing.

Rakmen propped his chin in his hands and stared out at the putrid bay. "Water skiing, my ass." The bullfrog let loose another torrent of gurgling croaks. A disturbing series of bangs came from inside. Something skittered in the underbrush on the other side of the car.

And Jacey screamed.

Not an I'm-ten-and-I'm-weird kind of scream. It was a Tower of Terror scream. Rakmen looked frantically for a bear. From inside the cabin, he heard a human-furniture collision as Mrs. Tatlas ran outside.

Jacey kept screaming and pointing at her leg as if it was about to fall off. "Whassat? Whassat? Whassat?" she howled. Two long, black worms squirmed in the oozy muck splattered over her pasty skin. One end stuck to her leg. The other flicked this way and that. Rakmen's flesh crawled at the sight of them.

"Shut up," he said, picking up a stick and poking one of the things. It was definitely stuck on her leg.

"What the heck is going on?" said Mrs. Tatlas, limping over.

"SOMETHING'S ON ME!" shrieked Jacey. "GET IT OFF!"

"Will you calm down. They're just leeches."

"LEECHES!!!"

Jacey was a tornado of arms and legs.

"I swear to God, you stop this right now," Mrs. Tatlas snapped. "I can't believe I practically broke my leg racing out here. You're freaking out about a couple of leeches." She swiped the muddy Kleenex out of Jacey's hand. "They can't be on very tight."

She gripped one with a Kleenex, wedged her thumbnail under the stuck part, and popped it off. Rakmen couldn't stop looking at the leech writhing on the ground—one moment long and thin, and then congealing into a gooey blob. Mrs. Tatlas dropped the second one beside the first, kicked pine needles over both of them, and went back into the cabin without a word.

"Look," Jacey said in a wobbly voice. "They left marks."

Two red circles the size of raindrops showed where the leeches had scraped through her skin with their sucky-mouths. Tiny drops of blood oozed out of pin-prick holes.

"Yuck," he said, squatting beside her and dabbing with a fresh Kleenex.

Her head drooped against his shoulder. "I hate it here."

"Me too," said Rakmen as he watched the leeches die in the dirt.

CHAPTER 11

If the lake was bad, the cabin was worse.

Rakmen stood with Jacey on the threshold, blinking as his eyes adjusted to the dim interior. Sunlight streamed through the doorway, illuminating Mrs. Tatlas's footprints in the dust. The ceiling sagged in the middle. So did the floor. The wall behind the pink Formica counter seemed on the verge of collapse. Crooked shelves bowed under the weight of more junk than Rakmen had seen in his life.

"Oh no," said Jacey, sliding her hand into his.

"It's not that bad," Mrs. Tatlas wheezed through a dust-induced coughing jag.

Piles of National Geographic magazines, their yellow spines faded to beige, towered in one corner next to a plaid recliner that oozed stuffing like pus. "A little cleaning," she continued, holding out a broom. "That's all it needs."

Her careful words were a thin sheet of ice over dark water. The look in her eyes unnerved Rakmen. Something in there had shaken loose. He wanted to sprint for the car, locking the doors behind him.

"Uh, Mrs. Tatlas . . ." He cast about for the right thing to say, the thing that would convince her they needed to go, and go now.

She closed her eyes and held up one hand. "Don't say anything. Please. Sweep."

He took the broom in silence.

There was no right thing to say.

Mrs. Tatlas turned her back and scrubbed at the filthy sink. Jacey moved toward her mother, but Rakmen pulled her back, the smell of Ajax stinging the inside of his nostrils. "Come on, Jacey. Help me move stuff."

Maybe if they left Mrs. Tatlas alone, the rattling bits would come back together. Rakmen swept to keep the panic down, wondering where she had put the car keys. The bristles of the broom scratched against the rough floor. Fear tugged at him. Even if he could get the car keys from Mrs. Tatlas, it wouldn't help. He didn't have his license yet, and it wasn't like he could make a break for it across the wilds of Canada.

Besides, he had Jacey to worry about. Her nose dribbled snot down her lip as she scooted chairs out of his way and held the dustpan to collect many years' accumulation of dirt, dried-up flies, and piles of mouse turds. The dust made them both sneeze. When she tugged on his sleeve to show him a basket full of collected birds' nests, her tears were gone. She was all twinkly-excited about the fragile eggs still nestled in the tiny cups of grass and moss.

"I'm going to get my camera," she whispered. "Okay?"

He nodded, and she scampered to the car.

If things had been different, Dora would be learning to crawl. Crawling would have turned to walking, and then she, too, would be bouncing through the world like Jacey—ebullient when everything else was going to shit.

Jacey returned, cradling the camera to her chest and sucking on a lock of hair. He was relieved to have her close in this strange place, but in the same breath, he wanted to push her away. She was not his sister.

He swept harder.

Jacey examined the over-burdened shelves and snapped pictures of warped glass jars brimming with buttons, bottle caps, and feathers.

At least five feet of wall space was strung with wire, from which hung hundreds of fishing lures, jangling quietly in the breeze from the open door. Jacey took pictures of all of them.

"We should go fishing later," Jacey announced.

Mrs. Tatlas frowned into the sink she was scrubbing.

Rakmen urged Jacey out of harm's way. "Come on. Let's do the bedrooms."

Flimsy walls separated the main room from the two back bedrooms and a closet-sized bathroom. The room on the left had a double bed with a broken headboard and a faded-to-gray quilt. The right had bunks—the top one so close to the ceiling that Rakmen felt claustrophobic looking at it—and a square window with a view of the swamp-lake.

"I get the top—" Jacey began. Then, bunks forgotten, she said, "Whoa. That's some wallpaper."

Someone had tacked scraps of map and bits of old newspaper articles on practically every visible bit of wall. Most of them were about record fish catches—35-pound trout, four-foot-long muskellunge, bass as big as porcupines—but there were also interviews with crotchety old-timers, accounts of crashed bush planes, and search-and-rescue alerts.

"Your uncle is cracked."

"He's my great-uncle," said Jacey.

Rakmen pulled out his notebook and scribbled down a headline about a string of bear break-ins at a nearby lake in 1973. "Major crime spree," he muttered. Uncle Leroy was clearly a whack-job, but Rakmen appreciated his need to remember.

Mrs. Tatlas leaned through the doorway.

Immediately, Rakmen felt short of breath, like the three of them took up every speck of dusty air in the place. Dirt smudged her face, but he could tell that she'd managed to tack her inner workings back together. He could breathe again. For now, at least.

"You okay with this room, Rakmen?"

"Sure," he said. "This guy's sense of style was amazing."

She tried to smile.

"What's the deal with this place anyway?" he asked.

"My uncle bought it in the '60s. He'd come up and fish. Once he retired, he spent most of the summer here. My brother and I used to come up all the time. But it was different."

"Like clean?" Jacey piped in.

"And with a lake?" said Rakmen.

"Cleaner," said Leah, glancing around and obviously dismayed by the clippings on the wall. "Things changed after his best fishing buddy died. As for the lake—" she said with a sigh. "There's an old dam at one end that was from back in the logging days. It probably gave way. That's why the water level is so much lower."

"That stinks," Jacey said.

And no one could disagree with that.

"I want a bunk!" Jacey announced, moving on to a new topic.

"You're sleeping with me in the other room," said Mrs. Tatlas, ignoring her daughter's spluttered protests. "Rakmen, can you set the mouse traps while we unload the rest of the car? Stuff's on the table."

Mouse traps. This deal was getting better every second.

As Mrs. Tatlas and Jacey hauled in their gear, started the propane fridge, and stashed boxes of cereal in large, metal, supposedly mouse-proof tins, Rakmen smeared Skippy peanut butter on the catch plate of each trap. After he'd set them, he tucked one in every place that seemed likely to appeal to mice—not that he had any experience with mice.

Jacey poked around the laden shelves, rattling jars of river rocks, and taking pictures of things she found interesting—a taxidermied mink, a snake skin that smelled of musk, a lone mitten.

"I don't wanna kill the mice," said Jacey, coming up behind him.

"Would you rather have them chew your face off at night?"

"Ew," she said, slugging him. "That's rats, right? Mice are kinda cute."

"Cute or not, I'm not sleeping with them."

"Me neither," said Mrs. Tatlas. "Ham and cheese sandwiches okay with everyone for dinner? I'm too tired to cook."

"Sure, Mrs. Tatlas," said Rakmen, screwing the lid on the peanut butter.

"Hey, Rakmen?"

"Yeah?"

She spread mayonnaise on six slices of bread. "I think you'd better call me Leah."

He stiffened. First names meant you had something in common "Okay," he stammered. Even though he was across the kitchen table from her, it felt too close.

She stopped arranging slices of lunch meat on sandwich halves and met his gaze. "I'm trying not to think about things at home." Her mouth turned up slightly. Around her eyes, she softened, and there was kindness there. "A long time ago, I was happy here. I'm hoping I can get some of that back."

He nodded, suddenly awkward, but wanting to believe her.

"I know this is strange," she said, "but we'll figure it out. I'm glad you came."

Rakmen nodded again. "I'm . . . I mean . . . I'll . . ." He tripped over the right thing to say. "I'll try to be helpful, Mrs. Tatlas—I mean, Leah."

Her name caught in his throat. She was the teacher. He was the student. That made sense, but ever since Promise House, those lines had blurred, and he didn't know where he stood anymore.

CHAPTER 12

Leah handed each of them a sandwich on a paper towel and grabbed a water bottle. "Let's go."

"Aren't we gonna eat here?" said Jacey, knocking on the water-stained table.

"I'm taking you to the point. It was always one of my favorite spots. Plus, you deserve proof that there's a real lake."

Rakmen followed them out of the cabin and along a tiny path, which hugged the shoreline. As Leah led the way, it seemed to Rakmen that her spine straightened and her head lifted. Maybe she really could leave Mrs. Tatlas behind.

"There's some moose droppings," she said, pointing to a pile of brown, marshmallow-sized ovals.

"Should we be worried about that?" Rakmen asked.

"No. It's not very fresh, and anyway they're really shy animals except during the fall."

"Why then?"

"The males get feisty during the rut."

Jacey made him stop and hold her sandwich so she could take a poop picture, and he could worry about moose survival strategies. Twenty feet ahead, the path nudged up against a ridge of grayish rock, which jutted into the lake like a huge, knobbly finger. Jacey clambered up and sat cross-legged on very end of the rocky point.

"It is a lake," she said as they sat down beside her.

From this vantage, Rakmen realized that Vesper Lake was shaped like a giant tadpole. Uncle Leroy's cabin was at the end of the long, swampy tail. The rest was open water ringed by forest. The sun setting behind them turned the surface bronze, and it was actually beautiful, as long as he didn't think about what might be in the water or in the deeply shadowed trees. Other cabins dotted the edge of the lake, all far enough apart to seem lonely. The one directly opposite perched crookedly on stilts. Its front windows reflected the sunset like huge, blank eyes.

"Look at the dock," said Jacey, pointing across the water to the cabin on stilts. A narrow lane of wood stuck out from the rocky shore in front of the building. "It looks like a tongue. The cabin is blowing a raspberry." She stuck her tongue right back, blowing spit.

"That is disgusting," he said.

The light was nearly gone. The surface of the lake turned from gold to blue-black. A light flickered on inside the tongue house. A shape moved behind the window and paused.

Rakmen shivered. Someone was watching them.

A warbling shriek rose across the lake. Jacey pressed against her mother. Rakmen scanned the area, cold rising in him. The call came again, closer this time, as if someone were trapped in a well.

"Is that a wolf?" asked Jacey in small voice.

"No, silly," said Leah.

The prolonged howl rose, fell, and ended in a choked gurgle.

"What is it?" Rakmen asked. No good could come out of sound like that.

"It's only a bird," she said. "A loon. See—over there."

Rakmen followed her finger. A black shape like a cross cut through the darkening sky. He could hear the whipping sound of its wings as it flew overhead.

"You should write that down in your notebook," said Jacey.

"Why?" The howling bird gave him the creeps.

"'Cause I couldn't take a picture fast enough," said Jacey, like that was totally obvious.

"You know," said Leah, "it might be fun to keep a bird list of all the species we see."

Rakmen wasn't convinced, but he pulled out his notebook, knowing Jacey wouldn't stop bugging him until he did it.

"What do you want me to say?" he asked.

"Howling bird," said Jacey.

"It's a common loon," said Leah. "That's the species."

Howling bird. Common loon. He tapped the pencil on the page before adding one more line. *Moose, maybe wolves. I don't know what is out here.*

* * *

Later that night, after he'd called his parents and pretended everything was fine, Rakmen lay in the bottom bunk, listening. Little claws scritched and scratched inside the walls. The night outside was full of trills and squeaks and rustling. He couldn't make sense of any of it. At home, he knew the difference between air brakes and an idling UPS truck. He could pick out fire trucks from police sirens. He could sleep through the occasional street fight.

But this . . .

A tiny, furry body raced across his pillow, grazing his cheek, and he flew out of bed so fast, he cracked his head against the top bunk. Giving up on sleep, he reached for his phone. Reception hovered around one bar of signal. His call home had been dropped three times, but he could probably get out a text. Only 11:30 here. Back home, Molly would still be up.

There is a rocking party going on here, he texted.

He sat on the edge of the bed in the dark, itchy and sweating. Damn mice probably had fleas. Rakmen wiped the sides of his face with a T-shirt. Everything about the cabin clung to him like a dirty film. He wished he could shed his skin and end up new.

His phone lit up as a reply came in, turning the underside of the bunk aquarium blue.

Uh? Good? That means you're having fun, right?

It's a midnight party of a million mice.

He hit send and heard the violent snap of a trap followed by a spine-chilling squeal from the front room.

Make that 999,999. There is not going to be water skiing.

Bummer. Swimming?

If you like leeches.

Maniacal hooting sounded across the lake. Another loon or maybe an owl.

At home, when he couldn't sleep, Rakmen would leave the house, easing the door shut so his parents wouldn't wake, and walk. Past the closed stores and deserted bars. Past the silent playground. Past the St. John's Bridge, its towers lost in the fog. The city at night was empty but not empty. You knew everyone was there behind all those closed doors.

OMG, Rakmen. You're torturing me. Tell me something good.

The hooting came again, closer now. This place was far from vacant. This darkness was full. But not with people. It was full of things he didn't understand. He wished he could explain this to Molly. Instead he typed **Jacey loves the camera.**

She sent a smiley face back.

She's taking pictures of everything. Even moose poop.

Hahahaha!

He smiled in the dark, psyched to have made her laugh.

Leah seems sort of better here. Like the place agrees with her.

You mean Mrs. Tatlas?

Yeah. She says we're not at school so I'm supposed to call her Leah. It's weird. How's SAT prep?

Rakmen imagined Molly cross-legged on the couch using a study workbook in her lap to conceal her sketchbook. If she were here, she could've drawn the view from the point with all the shadowed hillsides in dark charcoal.

groan

She would have added the loon in a black slash.

You'll rock it.

I'm trying. Hey, I've gotta run.

Rakmen squeezed the phone tighter, hating to break the connection. **'Kay. Miss you.**

Don't get lost.

He tucked the phone by the side of his pillow and lay back down, doubting he could get any more lost than he already was. He was both exhausted and wired, too antsy in the unfamiliar place to sleep. The mildew wafting out of his pillow made his throat scratchy. In the main room, mouse sounds erupted in fits and starts.

Over the rustling, he heard another noise. Leah was crying. The walls in this cabin were as thin as the ones at home, as thin as the door to the basement at Promise House. Leah cried like his mother, low and rhythmic, each sob catching in her chest. They cried because they were ground zero, and it was impossible for anything to rise from such toxic rubble.

Rakmen pulled the moldering pillow over his head.

He did not want to keep overhearing.

CHAPTER 13

The next morning, Rakmen stayed in bed as long as he could, eyes squeezed shut, trying to ignore the musty smell and the fact that he needed to piss. There was nothing good to get up for. Not one thing.

But he really had to piss.

He dragged himself out of the bunk, rubbing his eyes and wishing the day away before it even got started. Jacey was reading a fifteen-year-old National Geographic in the torn recliner. Leah stood in the kitchen. A mouse trap dangled in each hand, the lifeless mice splayed out like clumps of dryer lint.

"All the traps were full," she said. "Twelve mice."

Rakmen had heard every single one of them die in the wee hours of the night, and from the look of Leah's sunken eyes and hollow cheeks, so had she. "Uh, good? I guess."

"I guess." Leah turned in a futile circle, looking for some unknown thing, and then turned back to Rakmen with the traps still dangling.

"That's why we set them, right?"

"Yeah, right." She turned and headed out the front door. "I'll just . . . deal . . . with these last two."

He put two slices of bread in the toaster.

Nothing was different. He'd travelled three thousand miles from home and was still walking on eggshells and dodging blows. The only new thing was that he ate toast to the sound of scurrying feet.

Jacey abandoned her magazine and nabbed one of his slices.

"Hey," he said.

She stood with her back to him, studying the wall of fishing lures. "Hey, yourself."

Leah came back from the mouse graveyard and scrubbed her hands until Rakmen thought the skin might fall off. Jacey started at the top row of lures and touched each one in turn, all the way down. Leah poured cereal. Outside, that bird that sounded like it had swallowed a machine gun chattered its head off.

"Pileated woodpecker," said Leah in a slumped monotone.

"Uh...excuse me?" Rakmen asked. The air in the cabin was stifling.

"That bird calling. It's a woodpecker."

"Write it down," Jacey commanded, giving the last lure—a giant, red and white, spoonlike thing with jewel-eyes—a resounding flick with her thumb and third finger. It clanked against its neighbors. She wheeled around to face her mother.

"I want to go fishing."

"No." Leah's words remained flat, and there was something dangerous around her eyes.

"Look at these lures." Jacey flapped a hand toward the wall. "I bet they've caught a million fish. Come on. Take me fishing!"

"There's a lot to do here. Rakmen will take you later."

He very much doubted that.

Jacey let out a huffy whine.

The muscle in Leah's cheek tightened. "Give me a break, Jacey, I can't do everything."

"You don't do anything but lie around and cry."

"I am doing my best."

"You'd take Jordan." Jacey lobbed the words like a grenade.

Rakmen had the sensation that Leah's bones were giving way like buckled drywall and snapped girders. She set her cereal bowl on the counter with a thunk and walked into the bedroom.

Rakmen was on his feet before the door shut. "Come on," he said, grabbing Jacey by the arm. Between the very loose hold Leah seemed to have on herself and the prickly sensation that the dead were watching, he couldn't stay in the cabin another second.

"I want to go home," said Jacey as she let him tug her out the door.

If only he could make that happen.

"Why'd you have to talk about the baby?" he asked, when they'd circled around to the front of the cabin.

Jacey bared her teeth at him. "He's my brother! I can talk about him if I want."

"Yeah, but it doesn't do any good."

"It's called remembering," she snapped, picking up a pinecone and hurling into the lake.

"I'm not picking a fight with you," said Rakmen, picking up more cones and handing them to her. "But dead is dead."

"What if they're up there in heaven or something, looking down and thinking we forgot about them?"

A sludgy wave of pain rose in Rakmen's chest. As if forgetting were possible. He wished he hadn't eaten breakfast. "I'm saying that it upsets your mom."

Jacey threw the rest of the pinecones. When her ammunition was expended, she pointed to the shed attached to one side of the cabin. "Let's go explore that shed."

"It's probably full of wood," he said, but shrugged and followed her. Nothing else to do but count logs.

The morning sun sliced yellow fingers through the big trees around the cabin, and steam twisted up from the ground. The shed tilted ominously toward the water. Jacey pulled on the mildew-spotted tarp covering the doorway until the bungee cords holding it broke loose. She fell backward, ending up half-buried in the stinky plastic.

"This is so gross," she complained, "Get me out of here."

Rakmen ignored her and stared into the dim interior. Surrounded by piles of stacked firewood was a boat, upside-down on a pair of sawhorses. He whistled through his teeth; a long, low hiss of appreciation.

Even a city kid who knew jack about boats knew this was something special. Under a buttery layer of lacquer, the honey-colored wood of the hull glowed. Leaving Jacey to extricate herself, he skirted the stacks of wood and ran his finger over the smooth surface of its hull. "This boat is probably worth more than the whole cabin."

"It's a canoe," Jacey said, coming up beside him.

"Uh-huh . . . a canoe," he repeated, mesmerized by its graceful shape and the way the wood almost seemed alive.

Jacey got on her hands and knees and crawled under the canoe. "It's chained."

Rakmen squatted in the sawdust. Thin boards braced the inside of the canoe like ribs, and a crosspiece spanned the center. He tried lifting it off the sawhorses. A chain, looped around the boat's crosspiece and connected to an eye bolt screwed into the floor of the shed, rattled hoarsely.

Great-uncle Leroy was not as insane as he seemed. His cabin might be the biggest pile of crap Rakmen had ever seen, but he was safeguarding the best thing for miles around.

"Let's find the key," Rakmen suggested.

They tiptoed into the cabin. Leah was still in her room, and they were able to search without being seen. Behind the front door and near the pile of aged magazines, they found a hook on the wall. A key chain sporting a real scorpion encased in yellowed resin hung there. The single key was so old that the teeth were worn as smooth as beachside pebbles.

Jacey snatched it off the hook and tore her way back to the canoe, scrabbling under it with the scorpion in her teeth. The chain gave a deep rattle as she pulled it loose. She crawled out, spitting dust, and together they turned the canoe right side up.

"Let's carry it down to the water," Rakmen said, and bent to grasp the triangular, wooden piece set in his end of the canoe.

Jacey reached for her side, and then jumped back, squealing. A dime-sized spider clung to sheets of silk in the hollow at her end of the canoe.

"Come on," he said, exasperated.

The spider scurried to the other side of its web.

"Get it out."

"You get it out," he said.

Jacey sucked on her hair.

"Fine." Rakmen headed to her end of the canoe armed with a stick of kindling.

"Wait!" Jacey screeched, as he started to jab at the spider. She pulled the pink camera out of her pocket. "Take a picture first?"

"You want a picture of the spider?"

She nodded.

"Well, go ahead," he said, leaning back against the post of the shed. "I guess it's not any weirder than taking pictures of moose poop."

She shook her head violently.

"I thought you wanted a picture."

"Can you do it?"

He sighed. "Give it here."

Rakmen switched the camera to macro and leaned in close. Every hair on the spider's body stood out like brush bristles. Eight eyes, various sizes, shone like black pearls. Shiny fangs hung low between its front legs. He took a handful of pictures and then handed Jacey the camera.

"Put this inside the cabin and grab those life jackets your mom brought, okay?"

She wobbled off, scanning through the pictures as she went.

Rakmen used the stick to relocate the spider. As he was brushing out its web, his fingers grazed a tiny strip of weathered bronze screwed into the inside edge of the canoe. He felt his skin catch on something engraved upon the metal. He squinted at the tarnished letters in old-fashioned cursive.

Au large.

Rakmen breathed in swamp muck and rotting wood and stared at the words on the metal plate. They made him nervous. Like the owl in the night, they meant something, but he didn't know what.

Or whether that something was good or bad.

Au large.

Probably bad.

CHAPTER 14

Together they hauled the canoe to the edge of the water and slid it alongside a fallen log, gray with age, which bridged the muck and extended into deeper water. Balancing on the log, Rakmen guided the canoe out.

"Hold this while I get in."

"What if we flip?" Jacey asked.

Rakmen squeezed the bridge of his nose between thumb and forefinger. The musty smell of the Promise House basement filled his nose, and headlines from his notebook flashed through his mind. *Boy, seven, drowns in Clackamas River. Coast Guard calls off search for survivors of fishing boat.* "Put on your life jacket."

He tightened the blaze orange contraption around his own chest and lowered himself onto the front seat. Jacey balanced-beamed along the log. When she stepped in, the canoe wobbled wildly from side to side. Yelping, she plumped down on the rear seat. A bullfrog let loose a flatulent ribbit and slid under the surface, straight into the brown ooze, and they both white-knuckled the sides until the rocking ceased.

For the first ten feet, Rakmen used the paddle like a pole and shoved them forward. Stink rose from the rotting stuff at the bottom in bubbly explosions, but after a few more pushes, they slid out of the lily pads into deeper water.

Rakmen put his paddle in a stranglehold and reached forward with it. After a few strokes, the canoe veered off to the right. He switched sides, sending water drops in an arc above him. After another minute, they veered drastically the other way, and his arms hurt.

"People do this for fun?" he muttered, rubbing his arms.

Behind him, Jacey continued beating the water with her paddle. The canoe revolved a full three-sixty. This was worse than learning to drive a stick shift. While they fishtailed in slick zig-zags across the water, a breeze caught the canoe and blew them halfway across the main body of the lake. Each gust brought a new smell—pine pitch, wet earth, something spicy like cloves—and carried them toward the cabin with the tongue-like dock.

No matter how Rakmen paddled, the canoe shimmied erratically across the surface. He wanted to turn around and get back to shore, but waves sloshed against the sides of the canoe, pushing them along.

Looking up to gauge the distance to the dock, Rakmen saw a stout, gray-haired woman in jeans and a red sweatshirt emerge from the tongue house and walk down the steps to the dock. Again, Rakmen tried to control the direction of the canoe, paddling first on one side and then the other. Nothing he did changed their course.

Panic swirled through him. If they crashed into that dock, they'd flip for sure.

"Hey, kids!" the old woman yelled. "What do you think you're doing? Stop paddling." She crouched on the warped dock with more grace than Rakmen expected and caught the bow of the canoe before impact.

"Get up here," she growled, sliding the canoe parallel with the dock.

Jacey clambered out, and Rakmen followed. The woman nodded to him, indicating he should take one end of the canoe. "Let's pull it up on the dock so the waves don't damage Leroy's precious canoe."

That done, she sat heavily on a metal lawn chair with frayed nylon straps and scrutinized them. Her eyes glittered deep in a leathery face. Rakmen took a step back, feeling like a worm about to be snapped up. The end of the dock was at his heels. Jacey squeezed in close. The nylon of her life jacket swished against his side.

The old woman's eyes flicked to Jacey. "Quit chewing on your hair," she said. "Leroy said you had manners." Jacey gaped at her. "And close your mouth. You," she said, rounding on Rakmen, "are in the wrong damn place."

"Um . . ." Rakmen floundered for words. "You mean, like, trespassing?"

She laced her fingers together, flipped them around palm out, and pressed forward until her knuckles gave a staccato series of cracks. She rolled her eyes. "I mean, like, um . . . in like . . . the canoe." Rakmen's eyes narrowed, but before he could think of a comeback, she unlaced her fingers. "Neither of you has a clue what you are doing."

No good comeback for that either. It was true.

"Does Leroy know you stole his best canoe?" she asked, peering at them.

Rakmen stiffened. "I didn't steal it."

"He told us to come here and have a good time," said Jacey, bobbing up and down on her the balls of her feet, "so I figure he meant the canoe too. Keeps me out of the leeches."

At that the old woman leaned back in her chair and chuckled. "You're a funny one. I'm Edna Brackton, and I'm guessing you're Miss Jacey Tatlas."

"Yup."

"Leroy said you'd keep me on my toes."

Jacey squinted at her. "But you're sitting down."

Edna laughed again and spit off the side of the dock. "Who's the tall guy?" Rakmen wondered what Leroy would have to say about her manners.

Jacey grinned. "Rakmen."

Edna snorted. "Rock Man? That's a weird name."

"Whatever," he shrugged.

She squint-eyed him. "Well, whatever, I'm going to teach you how to paddle. This canoe," she said, stroking its graceful curves with one finger, "deserves better."

Her gibe reverberated in his head, as if she could see right through him and already found him lacking. From the trees behind Edna's cabin, a bird burst into an exuberant, rising trill. Edna whistled back. Instantly, the bird responded.

"You talk bird," said Jacey. "That's so cool."

Edna flashed her a smile, and not a sarcastic one either. "White-throated sparrow."

Jacey nudged him. "Write it down."

Edna waited for him to do something.

"What?" he asked.

"What?" she mimicked.

"Alright," he said to Jacey, pulling out the notebook and pencil. *White-throated sparrow.* "Now let's go."

"No. I wanna stay. She talks to birds!" Jacey said in a whisper half the lake could hear.

"Smart girl," said Edna, derailing his exit strategy, "Let's turn you into a paddler your Great-uncle Leroy won't disown. Put the canoe in the water," Edna commanded, pointing at him. He glared at her. She smiled back placidly.

Jacey tugged on his elbow. "Come on," she pleaded. "I want to know how to do it right."

"I'm not gonna say please," said Edna, "if that's what you're waiting for. Either you want to know how to paddle right or you don't."

Rakmen looked away from her. It was a long way back. He and Jacey had only ended up here because of the breeze, which was still blowing in the wrong direction. Between Edna's dock and the cabin were a hundred opportunities to drown.

With Jacey's help, he lowered the canoe into the water.

Edna presided from the lawn chair. "Hold the gunnel. That's what we call the edge of the canoe."

Rakmen curled his hands around the raised rim of the boat.

"First you have to know front from back," said Edna. "Look at the seats."

The two seats bolted under the gunnels were made of woven cane strips in a wooden frame. One was mounted only a few feet from the pointy end of the canoe. The other was much closer to the wooden bar in the middle of the boat.

"That's the bow," said Edna, pointing to the one with plenty of space. "The front. The lightest person sits there. The rear end is called the stern. That's where you sit," she said to Rakmen. "Get in," she said to Jacey, who hop-stepped into the front of the canoe, sending it into a dangerous tilt.

"Weight in the middle," Edna snapped. Jacey crouched. "Rock Man, put your hands on the dock and support yourself while you slide your butt into the middle. Keep your weight low."

When both of them were settled, she handed Jacey a paddle. "You—bow paddler—you are the power. Paddle, paddle, paddle. Always the same side. Always the same pace." Jacey nodded.

"And you—" The woman's head swiveled, owl-like, toward him. "You direct." She slashed an arm straight down, ending poker-straight and pointing west. "Here." She karate-chopped down again, now pointing ninety degrees from the first direction. "Or here. You decide direction. J-stroke and go there."

"J-stroke?" Rakmen asked, wondering if she would karate chop him next.

The woman snatched the paddle from him and turned on the dock so she was sitting alongside the edge and facing the same direction as he was.

"Like this." She grasped the rounded handgrip of the paddle in her right hand. Her left encircled the paddle shaft down near the blade. Leaning forward a little, she pointed the paddle in front of her with the flat blade facing the sky. She pulled it through the water until it was pointing straight down at the bottom of the lake, then she bent her wrist sharply. Rakmen watched as the paddle blade scooped the shape of the letter J in the water.

"Watch again."

They watched. Jacey, her face crinkled in concentration, started to put her hair in her mouth, but Edna glared at her, and she dropped it.

"The end of the stroke pushes the water away from you. You use the water."

"O-kaaay," Rakmen said. Watching this backwoods Yoda paddle from the side of the dock hadn't exactly cleared everything up.

"You try it now." Edna thrust the paddle at him, untied the canoe, and pushed them off before either Jacey or Rakmen could argue.

"I am the power. I am the power." Jacey muttered to herself in the bow. She bent to the task of pulling the blade through the water on the right side of the canoe.

Rakmen took a stroke on the left. Immediately the canoe veered right.

"J-stroke," Edna called.

He bent his wrist and banged the shaft of the paddle on the side of the canoe with a horrible clunk, but the canoe straightened. He tried again, this time putting more muscle into it. The canoe veered left.

"Too much!" Edna yelled from the dock.

Rakmen eased off the J part of the stroke until he found the exact amount of wrist flick that balanced Jacey's stroke and kept them straight.

"Ah-ha! The Rock Man does it!" the woman crowed from the dock.

Jacey stopped paddling and grinned over her shoulder at him. The canoe immediately veered right again.

"Hey you, Power," the woman yelled. "Do not stop!"

Jacey redoubled her efforts, showering him with water from her frenzied paddling.

"Hey!" yelped Rakmen.

"Sorry," said Jacey, through panting breaths. "Can't stop now."

Rakmen directed them straight ahead for twenty feet before adding extra wrist and turning the canoe toward the left. After another twenty feet, he turned again. They were pointing back toward the house.

"How do I turn the other way?" he hollered.

"No J," Edna called back.

He went back to a plain stroke and sure enough the canoe turned right in a wide graceful arc. The lake stretched out before them, sundappled and twinkly. Rakmen could see the rocky point where they had eaten dinner. Tall pines at its crest swayed in the breeze. Crisp, woodsy smells swirled past him.

There was some pattern to it all that he couldn't quite grasp. It was as if the sweep of the canoe drew everything together. A union of sky and water, stone and tree. There was order. Rakmen felt it but did not understand the way the pieces fit together.

CHAPTER 15

When he and Jacey skimmed to a halt at the dock, Edna beamed at them, and Rakmen couldn't help but smile back.

"Stay here a sec," said Edna, stumping back into her cabin.

Jacey waggled her eyebrows at Rakmen. "I'm the power! Did you see that? Did you see how fast we went?"

"Yeah, you did good."

Jacey glowed at him.

"Here ya go," said Edna, returning with a squashed yellow box of Nilla wafers.

"Oooh. Yum. I love these," said Jacey, taking a handful and passing the box back to Rakmen. He crunched into a cookie, reminded of his mom's banana cream pie. "That was so super!" Jacey jabbered. "Did you see how fast we went? My arms hurt a little. I like—"

"Listen," Edna cut her off, pointing to the shoreline down from the dock. Loud rustling punctuated by breaking twigs erupted from the forest. Rakmen stared into the bushes at the edge of the lake, crushing a forgotten Nilla wafer in one hand.

A huge shape was pushing through the branches.

Jacey grabbed at his sleeve.

"What in the—?" Rakmen muttered.

The shape emerged into sunlight. Not a bear shape or a moose shape. It was a canoe. Upside down. With legs. An arm snaked up over the top of the canoe and flipped it to the ground. A mud-splattered, bearded sasquatch of a man slung off a heavy backpack and began mopping sweat off his forehead with a wadded bandana.

The man threw back his head and drained his water bottle. When he was done drinking, he wiped his face with the back of his hand. Catching sight of them, he waved.

Jacey waved back.

Rakmen elbowed her. "Don't encourage him. He's probably homeless."

Edna busted into wheezing laughter.

"What?" Rakmen demanded.

Tears leaking from the sides of her eyes, Edna waved him off with one knobby hand. The crazy man loaded his canoe and sat on the bow seat facing backward. Within seconds he was skimming toward them, single-handedly propelling the canoe in a straight line.

"How's he doing that alone?" Rakmen asked.

Edna's laughter abated. "It's all in the J."

"Hey, there," said the man when he got close enough. "Gorgeous morning, isn't it?"

Edna nodded.

"Are you lost?" Jacey asked.

"Lost?" he chortled. "No way! I am living the dream."

Rakmen shifted on the rough boards of the dock. The guy looked like a meth head.

"How long you been out?" Edna asked him.

"Two weeks on trip. Now I'm heading straight for the boat landing and a double-scoop ice cream cone for breakfast." He leaned into his paddle stroke, the muscles in his back straining against his sweat-stained shirt. His beard shook as he grinned at them.

"Enjoy," said Edna as he skimmed by.

"I want ice cream for breakfast," Jacey whispered, awed into something like silence.

Rakmen watched the man paddle away. "What did he mean on trip? Like acid?"

Edna gaped at him, and then started laughing so hard she hacked up a glob of mucus. "On trip means canoe camping. That portage—the trail—it leads to a string of wilderness lakes."

"In the woods?"

"Of course."

"That's nuts. Why would anyone want to do that?"

Edna cracked up again, bending over her knees and shaking in her lawn chair. "You are a city boy, aren't you?"

Rakmen bristled. "Nothing wrong with that."

"No, I guess not," said Edna dryly, "if you're into that kind of thing. Me, I prefer the woods."

Rakmen watched the man paddle across the shifting surface of the lake. One moment it reflected cloud white and sky blue, the next a hundred different shades of green. The man didn't look anything like a meth head, Rakmen realized. He didn't jitter or twitch. He didn't look like he was about to jump out of his own skin.

And he didn't look homeless either, in spite of the unkempt hair and the grime. He wasn't a man who'd been chewed up and spit out. The bearded man paddled like home was a canoe, and he knew exactly where he was going.

• • •

It rained on and off—mostly on—for six days. Jacey had taken pictures of every piece of crap in the cabin—twice. Rakmen marked time in his notebook.

Tuesday: five mice.

Rain = even more mosquitos.

Cat piss stink in the woodshed. Leah says maybe bobcat. WTF?

Thursday: three mice.

Leech on canoe after we paddled to Edna's.

Will she ever stop talking?

Sandwiches. Mold on the bread.
Friday: three more furry corpses.
Everything smells like rot.

Leah stayed in her room most of the time reading and rereading a book called *Pilgrim at Tinker Creek*. When Jacey asked her if it was about Thanksgiving, Leah had answered, "It's about trying to make sense of the world."

"Sounds boring," said Jacey.

Sounds pointless, thought Rakmen.

Jacey found a box of ancient art supplies. A pad of cotton drawing paper, yellowed around the edges. A box of pipe cleaners in brown, green, and orange. A tray of dried and cracked watercolor paints. Drawing pencils. When she slathered bright smears of paint in the shape of turtles and rocket ships, it reminded him far too much of the basement at Promise House.

Only he couldn't leave after an hour.

Rakmen texted Molly and then paced the room trying not to text her. He read a battered booklet from the 1950s on how to thrive if confined to a bomb shelter for extended periods of time. Preparation is key! A Boy Scout manual on fishing from the same era depicted cheerful white boys crouched by streams and lovingly placing trout in wicker creels.

They both rummaged through the drawers and shelves filled with the detritus of Leroy's life. Rakmen found a folding knife, still sharp as anything, with the initials RJP on the handle.

"Who do you think this belonged to?" he asked, opening the blade and running a finger along it.

"Don't know," said Jacey. "Uncle Leroy's last name is Thoms. So he'd be *LT*."

As Rakmen replaced the knife in the drawer, his phone buzzed in his pocket, and he grinned to see Molly's name on the screen.

Guess what? she texted.

You're taking me skydiving when I get back?

Mom'll love that. Guess again.

He racked his brain for the most high-risk sports he could think of. Scuba diving? Ice climbing? Base jumping?

She doesn't let me walk around the block alone.

He set down the phone and felt the concrete setting up around his limbs. It always came back to the damage. Every joke, every chance they had to break free, Promise House caught them and held them. He wondered if he'd made her cry.

Rakmen swept up the phone again. **Sorry. Didn't mean to be a dick. I can't guess. Tell me.**

One of my drawings won an art contest.

!!!!!!!!!!!!!! Of course it did! You're amazing!

Blush.

Truth!

"Hey Rakmen," Jacey said. "Check this out."

Jacey's bugging me about something, he typed. **Catch you later?**

Yes! You must save me from utter boredom. :-)

He couldn't help smiling as he tucked the phone into his pocket.

Jacey was standing by the fishing lures holding up a pocket-sized notebook. "It's like yours."

"What's in it?"

"I dunno. A code or something."

Rakmen took it from her and flipped through the pages. Neat rows of tiny print filled line after line.

10 July 1959, 4 lbs 2 oz, 4 colors, silver Williams, w/ RJP

17 July 1959, 2 lbs 14 oz, 3.5 colors, black rooster tail, w/ RJP & EDB

The log began in 1958 and continued through 1977. Sometimes there were additional notes about weather or water conditions. Sometimes there were other initials, but mostly it was RJP and EDB.

"I think it's about fishing," he said. "See the weights?"

"Uncle Leroy really liked to fish."

That was an understatement. In the fifties, he and RJP must have fished all summer, every summer. In the sixties, the frequency dropped, weekends only. Then in the seventies it was erratic, a week here, a day there. The last page had three lines.

12 Sept 1977, 6 lbs 0 oz, 3 colors, Mepps gold spinner, w/ RJP

13 Sept 1977, 2 lbs, 5 oz, 2.5 colors, gold Williams, w/ RJP
26 Sept 1977

"That's weird," said Jacey. "What happened on September 26th?"

"Looks like he gave up fishing, I guess. We should eat lunch."

Jacey tucked the notebook back where she found it and helped him make sandwiches. When the sun came out in the middle of the afternoon, Jacey threw down a vintage National Geographic circa May 1984 and tugged Rakmen's arm. "Come on! Let's go exploring."

"Gimme a minute," he said, shrugging her off and finishing his text to Molly. **I'm sorry they won't let you go.** She'd been invited to the beach with a friend from school, but of course, her parents had said no.

I'm used to it. Bummed tho, she wrote back.

"Rakmen—" Jacey whined. "I want to go see Edna."

"Get us a water bottle and some bars and we'll go."

It's outdoor activity hour at Camp Fall Apart. Tiny dictator insists on a canoe ride, he texted.

Sounds like fun. Can I go to camp?

Even over text, he knew she was faking cheerful. He couldn't decide which of them had it worse. Molly's parents kept her home. His had sent him away.

Next summer for sure.

It's a date.

That sounded good to him.

Rakmen pulled their rain jackets off the coat hooks behind the door and waited while Jacey filled a water bottle. He itched to see the sun and get out of the cabin even if meant going to see grouchy old Edna. Anything was better than staying here.

Rakmen was half out the door with Jacey right behind him when a loud metallic bang exploded inside the wall behind the sink. Turning back toward the kitchen, he heard another ominous clunk and the deep gurgle of rushing water.

The bedroom door slammed open, and Leah stormed out. "What's going on? I'm trying to read."

Jacey glued herself to Rakmen.

The torrential sound of water increased.

Leah wrenched open the cabinet under the sink and shoved aside bottles of dish soap and bleach and stacks of old sponges. The moldy drywall behind the sink pipe ballooned outward, thrumming with the force behind it. Damp began seeping through, spreading out. They stared, transfixed. Then with a sloshy tearing sound, the wall gave way and gallons of rusty water poured onto the floor, soaking Leah's jeans.

"We're sinking!" Jacey shrieked.

"Not sinking, leaking," said Rakmen. "Where's the shutoff?"

Leah turned off the sink valve, but the water didn't stop.

"Get me a wrench," she hollered. "The water main is probably in the crawl space." She grabbed a flashlight and slopped through the growing puddle on the floor. Rakmen raced for the wall of tools in the shed out back. By the time he returned with the wrench, Leah had wriggled into the crawl space under the cabin.

Rakmen handed Leah the wrench and crawled in after her to hold the flashlight.

Jacey screamed through the floor. "It's getting worse. A chunk of the wall fell out!"

Leah strained against the valve. She smacked the pipe with the wrench and tried again. Groaning with effort, she pulled against the rusty plumbing.

Jacey hollered down another status report. "The rug is floating."

Rakmen touched Leah on the back. "Let me try."

She nodded and squeezed past him, trading the wrench for the flashlight, and he crawled forward into the muck. Rakmen pulled on the valve, putting his weight into it. With a screech, the valve fell into place. The sound of rushing water ceased, and in the dark confines of the crawl space, he could hear Leah cursing rhythmically.

"Come on," he said, half-pulling her out of the crawl space.

They waded through the main room and began cleaning up in silence. Leah mopped. Jacey filled a garbage bag with sodden masses of paper clippings. Rakmen hauled stacks of soaked magazines to the outdoor fire pit. Flecks of their yellow covers dotted his skin.

When he came back inside after the last load, Rakmen found Leah staring at a map on the wall. It was very old, navy blue with white lines delineating lakes and rivers. Dotted lines connected them, paths of some sort.

"I'm not staying in this mouse-infested junk heap," she said.

A prickling, electric sensation filled him. Rakmen tried to read the bend of her back, the tension across her shoulders. He wanted her to turn so he could read her face. Words couldn't be trusted.

"Good," said Jacey, a nervous smile twitching around her lips. "The cabin's yucky."

"Goddamn Leroy. He let everything go to hell," Leah said without turning.

They were teetering on the edge of something, but whether it was attack or retreat or surrender, he couldn't tell. In his pocket, his phone vibrated. Molly. Even if everything else at home was shit, Molly was there. The only bright spot. Rakmen decided to back retreat.

"We're ready to go," he said, keeping his voice as reasonable as possible. "Let's chalk this up to a bad idea. We can probably change our plane tickets." He didn't know what his parents would say about him coming back early. They didn't even have to know. Juan's mom would probably let him stay at their house.

Leah turned, her eyes narrowing. "That's not what I meant."

Rakmen had miscalculated. Again. Jacey trembled next to him, and he remembered the night Leah had broken the plates.

"We are not going home," Leah whispered. "We are going—" Rakmen strained to catch her words. "We're going *au large*."

Those were the words etched on the canoe.

Rakmen felt the ridged letters scraping his fingertips. *Au large* had sounded dangerous then and felt worse now. A sick, churning boil rose in his stomach. The lid that he'd kept so firmly clamped down was lifting, threatening his last shred of calm. Rakmen's hands balled into fists, but he forced himself to turn, to put one foot in front of the other, and to walk out the door.

CHAPTER 16

Jacey followed Rakmen.

"Stay with your mom," he warned.

She shook her head. "I'm staying with you."

And blam—they were back at Promise House, and she was asking him how to walk without a leg, and it was the middle of the night, and she was standing in the window of her broken-down house, begging him to bring her mother back.

He couldn't even save himself.

"Come on then," he growled.

They hauled the canoe to the water, and Rakmen paddled until the muscles in his arms burned and even then he didn't stop. He couldn't get far enough away from that woman's crazy. Not even the sun beating down on his shoulders could dislodge the dread he'd felt when Leah said *au large*.

The loud slam of a door echoed across the lake. Edna stood on her porch, hands on hips, evaluating the universe.

"Will you take me to see Edna?" Jacey asked in a small voice.

Small price to pay for the fact she hadn't spoken since they'd been on the water. Rakmen pointed the bow towards Edna, who was heading down to the dock with a fishing rod under one arm. As they approached, she settled herself into a folding chair.

"Hello, Power. Mr. Rock Man," she said, eyeing them closely. "Whatchya doing here? Why you got yellow crap all over you?"

"A pipe burst in the cabin," he said, scratching flakes of dried National Geographic off his arms.

"Everything got soaked," said Jacey, helping Rakmen tie the canoe to the dock.

"Leah need help?" Edna asked, without looking up from the worm she was skewering. Rakmen shook his head and sat down next to Edna, who added a red and white bobber to the line.

"What does *au large* mean?" Jacey asked, poking one finger in the margarine tub full of dirt and worms.

"That's what the old French trappers used to say before they headed out into the bush." Edna gave a mock salute and called out, "*Au large!*" The salutation rolled loudly over the surface of the lake.

In her gravelly voice, the words sounded almost cheerful. When Leah had said them, it felt like a grave.

"But," said Rakmen, "what's it mean?"

"Ah," said Edna. "That's the thing." Rakmen and Jacey leaned in. "It means to the wilderness. To the unknown. To adventure!"

"Adventure?" Rakmen repeated. Those words had nothing to do with that train wreck of a woman back at the cabin.

Edna cuffed him upside the head. "Look, mister. *Au large* is big. It's a way of life."

"I don't know what you're talking about," he said, rubbing his temple. "But Jacey's mom says she's leaving the cabin. Says she's going *au large*. Are you telling me she's planning to head to the woods like that crazy guy we saw?"

"Probably," said Edna, handing the fishing rod to Jacey and shooing her to the end of the dock. "Cast out by that submerged log."

Rakmen and Edna watched Jacey figure out the push-button reel. Her first cast was too jerky. The bobber splashed into the water ten feet from the end of the dock. "Go easy," Edna advised.

Once Jacey had successfully launched her worm out near the log,

Edna turned back to Rakmen. "Leah went 'on trip' a lot when she was a kid up here. Hell, I did too when I was younger. It's good for the soul."

"Whatever. She's a parent. She doesn't get to have an adventure because the pipes broke. Coming here was a bad idea. I think she needs to accept that."

"I think," Edna interrupted, "that you should give her some credit. I've talked to Leroy. I know about the baby." The sucker punch doubled him over. "She's struggling, and she's trying to figure it out."

"Jacey's scared of her," Rakmen said, lowering his voice and watching as the girl cast her worm out to its watery grave.

Edna nodded. "Grief is terrifying."

The bobber at the end of Jacey's line dipped under the surface, and she hooted, pulling back the rod. It curved, bouncing as the hooked fish struggled and broke free.

"The question is," said Edna, "what about you? Will you be going *au large*?"

Another adult who was so damn sure he could pick up the pieces.

"Like I have any say in the matter."

"You always got choices," Edna rasped.

"No, I don't," he said, feeling a sick bitterness run down the back of his throat. His sister was dead. He was stuck in the woods with a crazy woman, making sure she didn't get her other kid killed. He hadn't asked for any of this.

"You could blow your brains out."

Rakmen twisted to face her. Edna was staring across the lake at Leroy's cabin. Stone eyes. Clenched jaw. Wrinkled skin spread over a granite skull. She was all hardness. He fought the urge to recoil from the danger that had suddenly appeared. They shouldn't be here. He knew that now. But it was too late to get away.

"I don't think you're supposed to say that kind of thing," Rakmen stammered.

"Supposed to?" Edna asked. She shook her head, words bitter. "When the worst happens, stupid people say stupid things. I only say true things."

The blackness in her was loss.

It was emptiness.

In this moment, they were the same.

"Who did you lose?" Rakmen didn't mean to ask her, but the question escaped his lips. He saw the memory book from Promise House, the faces of children frozen in time. He needed to know.

"The three of us were best friends, Leroy, Richard, and me. We spent every summer on this lake together."

"You went fishing," he said, remembering the notebook and the initials.

She met his eyes, and her voice was softer than he had ever heard it. "We did a lot of fishing. Richard and I were going to get married. But he struggled something terrible with depression. I was young then and stupid and told him he didn't have an option. He had to get through it, shake it off . . ." Her voice trailed off and she rubbed the palms of her hands back and forth along the arms of the chair, breath slipping out of her.

"What happened?"

She stilled her hands and cleared her throat. "Let's just say he made a different choice." Her words were hard again. "And here we are, you and I," she continued. "Choices all around, Rock Man. Make one."

At the end of the dock, Jacey's rod bent double. She squealed and thrashed the rod in the air. "Fish! I got a fish!"

"Reel!" Edna commanded.

Jacey obeyed at top speed. She was flushed and panting by the time she had tugged an olive green fish as long as Rakmen's hand out of the water.

"Way to go, Power. You got a bass." Edna heaved herself out of the chair and pointed Rakmen toward a rusty metal bucket. "Fill that with lake water." She unhooked Jacey's fish and held it up by the lip for Jacey to admire.

"Oh, it's pretty."

Rakmen set the sloshing bucket beside her, and Edna dropped the fish in. She was back to normal, crusty and scarred over. A survivor.

The three of them were still watching the bass swim laps in the bucket when a mournful call reverberated across the lake. The loon had risen from deep water, shaking its head like a dog and sending water droplets in the air. Iridescent green shone on its head like an oil slick.

It turned and fixed a red-eyed stare on Rakmen. Warning shot through him, then the bird hooted, a soft feathery call which drifted over the lake. It dove, leaving nothing but a smooth spot on the water.

"Sometimes the Inuit buried their loved ones with a loon skull," said Edna, pulling out a fresh earthworm. "Supposedly the birds can see the way to the spirit world and guide the dead on their passing." The worm twisted around her gnarled fingers as she wove the hook through the middle of it.

Jacey looked up from the fish bucket. "What if someone doesn't have a loon skull?" she demanded.

"Huh?" Edna grunted, holding out the re-baited fishing rod.

Jacey ignored the rod and got in Edna's face. "If a person doesn't have a skull, will his spirit get lost?"

"I dunno. I haven't died yet." Rakmen wondered if Edna realized what Jacey was really asking. "Seen a lot a lost people, though," she continued, "and that's before they got buried." When Jacey didn't take the fishing rod, Edna put it down on the dock and started to pack up the tackle box. "I think you've got to find your own path."

"Do you know the way?" Jacey asked, expectant.

"I'm an old woman," Edna said. "I've been my own stern paddler for a long time. I won't be afraid when the loon comes for me. That's the ultimate *au large*." She pointed to the bass. "Whatchya gonna do with this thing? Clean it and eat it?"

Jacey shuddered. "No way. Let it go."

"Suit yourself," Edna shrugged.

Rakmen tipped the bucket over the edge of the lake and watched the bass swim to deeper water. The loon was down there with its blood-red eyes, watching. A chill swept through him.

Suddenly, he needed to get back. He needed to know which *au large* Leah had meant. Rakmen hustled Jacey into the canoe. Edna waved them off, and they paddled across the lake. The wind had shifted and a faint trace of rot rolled out of the bay where Leah waited in the moldy cabin. Its windows watched them approach, hollow-eyed and full of warning.

CHAPTER 17

The silence of the cabin as they approached sent fear racing through Rakmen. He pushed Jacey behind him on the trail that led up from the lake. If it was bad in there, as bad as he thought it could be, he didn't want her to see it first. Steam rose from the pile of soggy magazines in the fire pit.

The door was propped open.

Relief washed over him when he saw Leah hunched behind a small mountain of bundles heaped on the kitchen table. She was counting Ritz crackers into even stacks. Deranged but breathing.

"What's going on?" Rakmen asked.

"Packing."

"You're counting crackers."

"Yes. Twenty-six per lunch meal. Ten for you. Eight each for Jacey and me." Leah handed Jacey a tub of almonds, a measuring cup and a stack of plastic sandwich bags. "Put three-quarters of a cup in each bag. We need at least twelve plus another twelve of cashews."

Jacey's silence as she started measuring nuts told him she was equally nervous about the strange intensity that had replaced the vacancy in Leah's eyes. Rakmen wasn't sure which scared him more.

"Um, that's very precise," he prompted.

"Got to keep the weight down. We'll be out a long time, and we have to carry everything we'll need until our resupply stop."

Rakmen looked around the cabin. Soggy slabs of drywall hung from the hole under the sink. Soaked balls of lint and clumps of wet newspaper had collected in the low spots of the still-wet floor. Dark wetness had wicked up the upholstery of the couch.

A sudden image of himself with this crumbling cabin on his back flashed through Rakmen's mind. The weight would crush him. The stink rising from the cabin would suffocate him. He wanted to kick the walls until they collapsed. Instead, he pressed his palms against the table and forced his voice steady. "What's the plan here? Our agreement was eight weeks at this cabin."

"Well, it's a piece of crap. We need to get out of here."

"And by out you mean what exactly?"

"Twenty-four days on trip," Leah said, scrawling another line on her growing to-pack list. "We can carry enough food for twelve days if we're careful. I'll send a box to Branvin with enough for the return trip."

Jacey abandoned the nuts and watched them, wide-eyed.

"Trip? You mean camping?!" he said, unable to temper his rising voice.

Leah slammed the pen down on the table. "Yes, camping. We paddle across the lake, carry the canoe over to the next one, and keep going. Come on, Rakmen, this isn't rocket science."

"No," he said, pressing hard against the tabletop. "This is insane. We can't disappear into the woods. What about Jacey? You'd let her get eaten by wolves?"

"Wolves?" Leah asked, looking at him like he'd grown a third eyeball. "Are you serious? I think you watch too many movies. Jacey, see if there are sleeping bags in that closet."

Jacey scurried toward the tower of camping gear visible behind an open door.

"You can't do this," Rakmen said, panic rising. "We'll end up like that guy who cut off his own arm or the kid who died in the bus in Alaska. You'll get us killed."

Leah burst to her feet like he'd electrocuted her. The chair slammed into the wall as it flew backwards. "Shut up!" she yelled. "We're not going to die!"

"You don't know that!"

Her jaw clenched and anger darkened her eyes. "You can stay here, but Jacey and I are going."

Behind him, Jacey began to cry.

"I can't stay here," Rakmen hollered back. "This place is wrecked."

Leah threw her hands in the air. "Then come, but shut up about it."

The room seemed to swirl and tilt around him. A nightmare queasiness filled his gut.

"I can't come. I don't know how to do anything. I don't even know how to use this." Rakmen picked up the GPS unit Molly had given him and shook it at her.

Leah's face twisted violently. She clawed the device from his hand and flung it across the room. It hit the corner of the wood stove and thudded to the floor. Shoulders heaving, she caught her breath. "I'm sorry. I shouldn't have done that."

Jacey picked up the GPS and held it out to Rakmen. The display was a web of cracks. Calm swept over Rakmen. He wasn't getting sucked down like this. Not with her. Not even for Jacey. Without a word, he turned and walked out of the cabin. Bright sun spiked through the trees, dazzling and disorienting. He turned, unthinking, and took the path toward the point, breaking from the trees like an unconscious man resurfacing.

In crisp flashes, like the shutter click on Jacey's camera, he grappled for something solid. The gray granite rock of the point. The solid blue sky like the inside of a bowl. Heat from the sun on his head and neck. Choices all around. Make one. That's what Edna had said.

Rakmen pulled out his phone and dialed home.

It was time to go. He'd given this a fair shot but it was over.

"Hi, Mom. It's me."

"Oh—how are you, *mijo*?" She exhaled the greeting, vaporous and thin. "Tell me something good."

He wanted to cry. Rakmen forced down the lump in his throat. "Um . . . it's a beautiful day here. Very sunny." He couldn't help it. He had to save them from himself, and he hated it.

"Nice," she said. "What else?"

"Jacey caught a bass."

His mother murmured her approval.

Rakmen pressed the phone more firmly to his ear, wondering how to tell her that he needed a flight home, and he needed it now. "Mom, what's going on? You sound really out of it."

"Oh—" she said again.

"Mom, are you sick?"

"No, I'm not sick. I'm not sure how to tell you this over the phone." He held his breath. Rakmen didn't want to be told anything. "Your dad is moving out for a while."

The air pressure around him seemed to change. "I don't understand."

"We're separating. It's been so hard since Dora . . . Look, Rakmen, I can't talk more now. Your dad and I have decided to try it apart for a while, and then we'll see about getting back together. I don't know any more than that."

Rakmen squeezed his eyes shut and pinched the bridge of his nose. He knew without asking that his mom was sitting at the desk in front of Dora's picture. Everything spun back to that tiny person. She'd sent them hurtling into space. Her explosion was blasting everything apart. "I don't know what to say, Mom."

"Oh, *mi amor*, me neither. It's not your fault." He wished he could incinerate on the spot. If he'd watched harder . . . if he'd known better . . . "Look, sweetie," she continued, "we'll be okay. It does me a world of good to know you're in a nice place and having fun. I'm so proud of the way you take care of Jacey. She needs a brother like you."

"Mom, I need—"

"Leah told me how sweet you've been. I'm really proud. I'll see you at the end of the summer, okay?"

"Yeah. The end of the summer. Sure."

When she ended the call, Rakmen stood holding the phone for a long time. A breeze ruffled the surface of the lake, breaking the reflected trees into shifting splinters of green and brown. Across the water, he could see the place the ice cream guy had emerged from the woods, muddy, stinking of sweat and—incomprehensibly—grinning.

He had smiled and said it was glorious out there.

To the north and to the east from the rocky point where Rakmen stood, the forest spread to the horizon in a shifting patchwork of green.

He would go.

Not because Jacey needed him or because Leah did or because his mother wanted to believe he was weaving her a goddamn basket at summer camp. But because all around him, houses were collapsing, and maybe it was better to be where there were no houses at all.

CHAPTER 18

Rakmen sat on his bunk and fiddled with the GPS. It powered up, but the display was shot. *Don't get lost.* That's what Molly said at the end of each conversation they'd had since he'd been up here. He hadn't been able to bring himself to tell her about the GPS.

Or about going *au large*.

For four days, Leah had been in a packing frenzy, attacking her crumpled list with a red pencil every time she added something to the carefully measured bags of almonds and all their other gear. Somewhere in the pile was the green nylon bag with his clothes for the trip. Rakmen was still trying to block out the cringe-worthy moment when he'd had to itemize its contents for her and take out some underwear—four boxer briefs were apparently the maximum allotment.

But he had to tell Molly something, and soon. He swiped the phone off the bedside table and slammed out a text.

Long time, no see.

While Leah had packed, Rakmen had spent as much time as possible with Edna. Partly to avoid another blowout, but also because Edna was putting him through his paces, showing him the things he needed to know to survive this trip. And of course, Jacey had stayed stuck to him like a shadow.

His phone beeped.

How's the water skiing?

Beyond epic except when my skis get stuck in the moose muck.

Moose muck?

It's as bad as it sounds.

grin

Jacey pushed through the door and plopped on the bed beside him. "Whatchya doing?"

"That door was closed," he said, frowning at her.

She shrugged, pushed her pink camera into his face, and took a picture. "Mom says we're leaving in a half an hour."

"Go on," he said, batting her away, "I'm texting Molly."

Jacey pursed her lips and made kissy noises as she left.

I'm gonna be out of touch for a while.

??? He could practically see her brow furrowing, the scar puckering.

We're going on a canoe trip for a few weeks. Even typing the words sent worry jittering through him. At least he sounded like he had his shit together in text.

I don't understand.

Rakmen ran his fingers through his hair. Text wasn't so safe after all. She was already worried. Outside, frogs were going crazy in the lily pads, and Leah was hollering at Jacey to take their paddles down to the shore.

He should walk right out of here. He could hitchhike to Toronto and get a standby flight. Rakmen sagged back on the bed. He would be a minor crossing an international border alone. Good luck with that.

The phone in his hand rang, and Molly's picture popped up on the screen. He cursed under his breath. Text was hard enough. He wasn't sure he could keep it together in real time.

"Hey there," he said, switching hands so he could wipe the sweat from his palm.

"What's going on?" Molly wasn't clueless about Leah, of course.

"Well," he said, realizing that even though he wanted to tell Molly, there weren't words for the way all the falling-apart-things had pushed him off this particular cliff. He took a deep breath and started again. "We decided to go camping. There's this amazing canoe here, and there are trails and lakes and stuff. Exploring around, you know."

"Yeah, I guess," said Molly, dubious. "You want to do this?"

"Jacey's really excited."

"I'll bet."

In the silence that followed, Jacey poked her head in. "Time to go."

He nodded and held up one hand to shush her.

"Will you be able to text me?" Molly asked.

"About that," said Rakmen, shifting on the bunk. "There won't be phone service out there. That's why I wanted to let you know. So you won't worry." He cringed, glad that she couldn't see him trying so hard to put on a good show.

"I will anyway."

He forced a laugh. "Don't."

He would worry enough for both of them.

"You've got the GPS, right?" she asked, trying to match his fake cheerfulness with her own.

Rakmen stared down at the cracked screen. "Yup. I've got it."

"Don't get lost."

He wanted to promise her that he'd come back safe, but they would both know that was a lie. "Molly, I've got to go. I miss you."

"Right. Me too. Bye."

A sick sourness rose in him as he ended the call, powered down his phone, and left the GPS on his bunk. He felt naked and unmoored, as if nothing tethered him down any more.

Leah and Jacey waited in the main room. Their three packs— small, medium, and behemoth—were lined up next to the door.

"I've weighed them," said Leah, the past few sleepless nights all over her face. "Twenty-six pounds for Jacey. Yours is thirty, plus the canoe makes about eighty. Sixty-nine pounds for me. I guess we're ready to carry them down."

Rakmen avoided looking at her, hoping that would quell his urge to kick the legs off the table. It didn't help. To save the furniture, he carried the packs to the canoe waiting on the shore. Jacey circled their pile of gear taking pictures. He ducked his head to avoid her view-finder. He lifted the canoe into the water. When the gear was stowed to Leah's precise specifications, she waved him toward the bow seat.

Rakmen didn't move.

"Come on," Leah snapped. "I want to get moving."

Half of him wanted to shuffle to the bow and be done with it, but the other half fought back. "That's not my seat."

Hard lines rose on her face. He could almost hear the joints freezing up. "I really think you should let me paddle stern," she said, through clenched jaws.

Jacey stiffened. "Edna says he's the direction."

"Then why's he wasting his time babysitting you?" Leah snarled.

Jacey scowled up at her, and for a second, Rakmen thought Leah might slap her. He stepped between them, and tried to chan-nel his father's confident nurse voice. "Edna said the heaviest person should be in the stern. I can paddle there fine and then you can lead the way from the bow. Read the map and stuff. Tell me where to go."

Jacey squirmed behind him. "I'm the power," she whispered, "in the bow."

He didn't wait for Leah to respond. Keeping them moving for-ward was his only concern now. Stopping felt more dangerous than staying put. "You're in the middle, Power," he said, urging Jacey into the canoe and settling her on the large pack in the middle. "From here you can keep an eye on me. Make sure I'm doing it right, okay? And be in charge of the snacks."

She grinned at him.

"Get in," he said, looking at Leah. "Please." He held the canoe steady.

Leah studied him for a long moment before getting in the bow. Whether she believed him or was saving the fight for later, he didn't know. But maybe it didn't matter. As soon as they were all in place, Rak-men poled through the mucky shallows and sent the canoe skimming out into open water. He squinted against the bright sun as he paddled into its brightness. A breeze rippled across the surface of the lake, turning it into a sparkling patchwork of green and gold and blue.

As they sailed past Edna's dock, a loon rose ten feet off the bow, fixed them in its red stare, and then dove again. Rakmen's stomach pitched as he imagined the canoe rising bow first from the water like a porpoise and following the bird into the depths. They were almost to the portage when a hoarse cry sounded behind them.

"It's Edna!" Jacey squealed, thrusting her paddle in the air and waving it in salute. The stout woman on the dock waved back.

"Bye!" Jacey shrieked.

From across the water, he heard Edna call, *"Au large!"*

CHAPTER 19

Three more strokes and the canoe slid into the sandy shore with a crunch. Leah climbed out and straddled the front of the canoe to stabilize it while they unloaded. "Jacey, hand me your pack and then climb out. Keep your weight in the middle."

"I know that," Jacey snapped. "Edna showed me."

Rakmen rolled the shaft of his paddle crosswise on his knees, waiting for his turn to get out. "Okay," Leah said, nodding to him. "Climb over the big pack and when you get past it, lift it out."

Rakmen handed her his paddle and lifted the monstrous pack. On shore, Leah strapped their paddles to the sides of the backpack. Rakmen sat on a log, retied his boots, and flipped to a fresh page in his notebook. Underneath today's date, he wrote *au large*. Edna's farewell had lodged in his throat, choking him. If he were braver, maybe he'd feel excited. If he believed he was leaving his troubles behind, maybe he'd want to go. But he wasn't brave, and he didn't believe.

Jacey slid next to him. "Look what I found," she said, holding out a handful of jagged, nearly-translucent pebbles. "Do you think they're diamonds?"

Looking up from the patch of rocky beach between his feet seemed to Rakmen to take an extraordinary amount of effort. He shook his head. Her face drooped, and he tried to rally. "They're really cool, though. I like this one best."

Happy again, she bounced off the log and held out her hand to Leah.

"Quartz," said Leah and went back to wrestling with the straps on the pack.

Jacey bobbed up and down. "Can I have a bag for them?"

Annoyed, Leah wiped a sheen of sweat from her forehead. "You can't take them. These packs are heavy enough already."

Rakmen watched the pep drain out of Jacey. "But—"

"No."

That was that.

Leah double-checked that the canoe was empty.

Jacey gazed at the glittering rocks in her hand. At snail speed, she began to line them up one by one on the log. Rakmen gave a low whistle. When she looked up, he held open the cargo pocket on his pants and jerked his head toward it. Grinning, Jacey scooped up the discarded treasures and hid them safe in his pocket.

They were ready for orders.

"Here," said Leah, holding up the small pack so Jacey could stick her arms through the straps. "Let me adjust them for you." A few tugs and Leah was satisfied.

"Can I go? Can I go?" Jacey bobbed up and down on her feet.

"Wait. We stay together." Leah tightened one more strap. "Rakmen, help me with this, then I'll help you with the canoe."

Lifting from behind, Rakmen hoisted the pack into the air. It was going to crush the scrawny woman like a bug. Leah shrugged into the shoulder straps, clipped the waist belt, and pulled a strap that she called a tumpline onto her forehead.

"That looks like agony," he said.

Leah grunted and her expression, if possible, grew even more pained.

Perhaps that was the point. To suffer.

"Alright," she grunted, "you have to flip the canoe. I'll hold one end up while you get under it."

Rakmen waved her off and slid the mid-sized pack on. "I got this."

"No, you don't got this," Leah spluttered.

Ignoring her, Rakmen grabbed the center thwart of the canoe in his left hand and the far gunnel with his right. He pulled the canoe off the ground, slid it up his left thigh, and with smooth, quick motion flipped it upside down over his head. Thank you, Edna, he thought as the yoke of the thwart settled into place on his shoulders.

He stole a peek at Leah from under the canoe. Her expression made it clear he'd earned an A+ in canoe lifting.

"I'm impressed. Who taught you that?"

"Edna!" Jacey squealed.

"When did you . . . How? Oh, never mind," said Leah, throwing up her hands. "I kind of love that old bat."

A yellow sign fixed to one of the trees had a picture of a person with a canoe on his head—Rakmen nodded a salute to his silhouetted compatriot—and the words *Vesper Lake to Wren Lake 375 meters*. That was a lap around the track at school. Piece of cake. He could do this. But Rakmen's load felt like a Mack truck. Three seventy-five might turn out to be a hell of a lot longer than it sounded.

"This is the shake-down run. Let's stick together," said Leah as she started up a series of natural stone steps leading from the sand where they'd unloaded to the trail leading into the forest. Jacey trotted along behind her.

When Rakmen took the first step, the canoe's center of gravity shifted, and the stern dug into the dirt. He overcorrected, and the bow hit one of the rocks in front of him with a bang. He panted, shifting the canoe on his shoulders until it felt stable.

One step.

That's all he'd managed, and his shoulders were already burning from the weight of the canoe and the straps of the pack. All the practice time with Edna had made him think he could do this. Now he wasn't sure. But staring down at the rough gray rock under his feet, Rakmen realized it was this—one step at a time—or go back to the moldy, flooded cabin full of mice.

Forward.

Or blow your brains out.

He slid his hand along the gunnel to stabilize the canoe before taking a slow, steady step up to the next rock. By the time he reached the level portion of the path, his thighs were burning, and his spine felt compressed. Everything was against him, even gravity.

The portage was narrow and covered with rusty orange pine needles from the huge trees on all sides. They were springy underfoot and muffled the sound of his steps. He wondered what other sounds were silenced by this forest. He wished he could see, but the canoe enclosed his head almost as fully as a bag over a hostage's head. He could see the bow seat, the golden ribs of the canoe, the trail, and the slip of metal that read *au large*.

The words pounded through his head as he walked.

Au large. Au large. Au large.

He trudged to their drumbeat.

Sweat trickled down his face and stung his eyes.

The trees changed from huge pines to a kind that grew very close together, making a dark tunnel around the trail. He began to feel afraid. His ears strained to detect movement. Bears. Wolves. Whatever lurked in this place without road signs or rest stops or ambulances. Trapped under the canoe, he imagined them coming for him, burying their muzzles in his flesh.

Rakmen caught the toe of his boot on an exposed root. He lurched to the left. The canoe slipped, unbalancing him further. He lunged to the right to compensate, slipped on an exposed rock and went down on one knee still underneath the bulk of the canoe. The bow caught in a low branch beside the trail and held. Rakmen sucked air into his lungs as adrenaline surged through him.

They could come now. The wild animals. They could bring their fangs and claws. A welcome alternative to this pain, this humiliation. But they didn't, and before long, Rakmen's thighs began to cramp from crouching under the canoe. He forced himself to stand, pushing the canoe up with him. The bow squealed against the slender branches as it pulled free, snapping twigs and filling the air with the tangy smell of pitch.

He had to go on.

Au large. Au large. Au large.

He picked his way through a rocky section of trail.

Pins and needles darted through his hands from holding them at face-level. The knee that had hit the ground throbbed. His leg muscles ached and his bruised shoulders reverberated with pain at every step.

He hated the canoe.

He hated the rocky ground.

He hated the hot, rot-filled air that filled his lungs.

Three hundred seventy-five meters was infinity.

It seemed he would always be lurching forward under this unbearable weight. There was no job at Ray's auto parts shop. There was no family to go home to. There was no driver's license, no car, no college, no girlfriend, no bright shiny future self.

Only this.

Au large, au large, au large.

The pain of it. The punishment.

The big hollow inside of the canoe was an echo chamber for his worst thoughts. He deserved this. He was an asshole for thinking that taking care of Jacey would make up for failing Dora. Slick with sweat and aching everywhere, he knew that was stupid. He didn't do things right. Ever. He was wrong. So many ways wrong.

Au large, au large, au large.

God—

The screaming in his head was making him crazy. He would soon be deafened by the noise if he didn't silence his mind. He had to cross 375.

One, two, three . . .

Rakmen began counting steps. He got to a hundred and started over.

CHAPTER 20

He felt the next lake before he saw it.

A whisper of breeze slipped under the canoe, licking the sweat from his neck. He smelled wet earth, fresh enough to overpower his own stink. A glitter of water showed between the ground and the canoe.

With his last ounce of energy, Rakmen pushed the canoe up over his head, eased it into the crook of his arm, rested it on his thigh, and slid it down to the shore. Edna should have told him how goddamn much this would hurt. He kneaded his shoulders and looked around, grateful for the three hundred and sixty degree view and his release from the echo chamber.

Wren Lake was far bigger than Vesper Lake, and it was a proper lake, not swampy at the edges. Jacey had peeled off her boots and was wading in the shallows. Leah had dropped her pack on the bank and was gulping down water. Circles of perspiration spread across the armpits of her T-shirt.

Rakmen knelt, splashed water on his face, and pulled up his pant leg to look at his knee, which was oozing blood.

"How did that canoe carry?" Leah asked.

He dropped his pants leg. What he wanted to say was like crap. Instead he shrugged.

"I know," she said. "It was awful. My pack is a beast too. At least you're not an out-of-shape teacher. Here." She tossed him a piece of chocolate along with a feeble grin.

Jacey stood next to him, hands on hips, while he unwrapped the slightly squishy brick of candy. "You were slow."

He slumped to the ground and let the chocolate melt in his mouth. "You carry it next time."

Jacey sat next to him and leaned on his shoulder. "It's too heavy for me."

He looked down at the top of her head. Her part was jagged. A wild tangle stuck out on one side. A bit of leaf was lodged near her left ear.

"I thought you were the power," he said, surprised to find that he felt grateful that she was sitting near him.

"Well, yeah," she said, "but I'm short-range."

"Short, for sure."

"Hey!" Jacey grinned at him, a smear of chocolate on one cheek. Sweat beaded on her forehead, and she was flushed with the effort of the trail, but she bounced with excitement.

Rakmen didn't know much about little girls, but even he could see that this one was happy. In the middle of bloody, painful *au large*, Jacey was blissed out.

He didn't get it, but—he had to admit—he kind of wanted to understand.

• • •

The rest of the day was a blur of lake and trail. As Rakmen lifted the canoe on the last portage, a blister on the palm of one hand burst, and the fluid inside it splattered his face. He didn't have the strength to do anything but register how gross that was, add the spiking pain to his list, and hit the trail.

He'd always associated that phrase, hit the trail, with cowboys, but after five portages, he now understood it to mean the dazed, aching, echoing state in which all you wanted to do was beat the ground with your fists in frustration. A hundred times that day he'd considered lying in the path and refusing to move, but something had kept him going— whether it was hating Leah or hating life or just following Jacey.

He watched his footing. The last thing he needed was to fall again. From the wet, warm slick of blood, Rakmen could tell the scrape on his knee had reopened. With his luck, he'd probably break something if he fell again, and of course, they had no phone.

Mechanically, he set down the canoe, hefted Leah's pack, and loaded it in the bottom of the boat. Jacey had long since stopped slipping rocks into his cargo pockets. She sat on a rock at the edge of this new lake and stared blankly out into the growing dusk.

Leah handed him the smaller packs. "We made it, guys."

Rakmen grunted. All he wanted to know was when he could lie down. Instead he stood and waited for Leah and Jacey to get in the canoe. Sitting down would be the end of him.

As he picked up the paddle and thrust the canoe into deeper water, his open blister burned against the wooden shaft, and every muscle in his arms and torso screamed in protest. *Au large* was the perfect torture, he thought. When you can't walk anymore, you paddle. When your hands are about to fall off, you hike. And every single part of your body ends up hurting.

But it had also, he realized, turned off his brain. It had been hours since he had thought of home or Dora or the gaping shotgun blast through his chest. The pain in his body trumped all of it. Its stupor was a small but not insignificant treasure, like the nuggets of quartz in the pocket of his pants.

When Leah pointed to an open campsite, he added extra force to his J-stroke and nosed the canoe into shore. The sun had dropped below the horizon, and dark was coming fast now. The spot was mostly rocky, with a grassy oval in the middle. Some other camper had made a ring of stones for a fire, and a twisted grill leaned against it. Rakmen hauled up the big pack, eyeing the line of dark trees behind the campsite. He didn't like the way the forest pressed against them.

"Hey, Jacey," said Leah, emerging from the open top of the huge pack with a collapsible saw, "I saw a downed cedar along the shoreline. Let's go get some firewood. Rakmen, can you find the tents?"

He nodded and watched them disappear around a rocky point. When the sound of Jacey's voice faded, other sounds filled his ears—swishing, creaking, tapping. He had no idea what this place contained. He unpacked their gear, glancing over his shoulder every few minutes. Two tents—one blue and one orange, sleeping bags and pads, the nylon sacks that held their clothes. All the crap he'd been carrying. He found the red zippered pouch that held the first-aid kit and rummaged through it for three Advil and a Band-Aid.

"You're bleeding," said Jacey, coming up behind him and dropping an armload of wood.

"Don't sneak up on me."

She grinned. "Wasn't sneaking. I was quiet. Now gimme that." Jacey swiped the Band-Aid out of his hand and insisted on wiping down his knee with an alcohol pad.

Too exhausted to argue, he let her fuss over him. "I didn't think you knew how to be quiet." She made a show of gluing her lips tight together. "I'll believe it when I see it," said Rakmen.

Silence didn't last long. As soon as Leah returned to camp with her own armload of small branches, Jacey returned to a running commentary on the sound of frogs and what kind you could eat, whether cattail roots tasted like celery, and if leeches ever ate anything besides blood.

"Come on," he said, pulling her away from the fire pit where Leah was lighting a fire. "You need to chill out. Let's put up the tents."

"Have you ever slept in a tent? I'm so excited. It's like a little fort."

The thin nylon was no substitute for proper walls. Tired as he was, Rakmen wondered if he would be able to sleep. The ever increasing dark seemed to amplify the sounds around them, and the flickering light from the fire cast a pitifully small circle of brightness. If anything, it made the dark seem darker. It was as bad as being under the canoe.

Or in the basement of Promise House.

By the time they had finished, the water for their dehydrated food packs had boiled. "Here," said Leah, handing them each a bowl of glop.

He tipped it toward the firelight, trying to figure out what color it was.

"It looks gross," Jacey whined. "What is it?"

"Lasagna."

Rakmen stole a glance at Leah, wondering if she was going to yell at Jacey, but his biology teacher was out of steam. She stared at the fire, spooning in mouthfuls of glop. Rakmen stuck his spoon in the bowl. His dad made terrific lasagna, and it came out of the pan in thick, cheesy squares. It did not resemble this stew of noodle bits, red sauce, and rehydrated beef crumbles.

The fire crackled and popped. All around the campsite, trees swayed and leaves rustled. He was a city boy overdosed on green and pain. Rakmen's stomach rumbled. He chewed slowly at first, and then more quickly. The sauce was tangy and full of garlic. Soon he was shoveling the noodle mash into his mouth, amazed that anything could taste so good. Especially something that came out of a foil packet looking like lumpy dirt.

"This is delicious," said Jacey, her words garbled by the half-chewed food in her mouth.

Leah nodded and kept eating.

As his belly filled with hot food, the aches and pains in his body dulled. Jacey threw a pinecone on the fire. It spluttered and then burst into flame, throwing sparks. She hummed under her breath and poked at the coals. The flickering light from the fire transformed her features. She was no longer a dull smudge of a girl. She was glowing and otherworldly.

When Jacey caught him looking, she smiled.

That look again.

The look that said he was enough. More than enough.

She was wrong, of course. But he felt satiated somehow by the food and the fire and the cessation of labor and by having her close.

Maybe it was animal nature to survive. A paleo thing—all burning torches and red paint on cave walls.

When they finished eating, Leah handed him a head lamp. "I need you to help hang the food pack."

He took the head lamp but stared dumbly at her. "Hang it?"

"In case of bears."

"I thought you said we'd be lucky to see a bear because there aren't many of them." Fighting a bear for their silver packets of dehydrated food was definitely beyond the limits of Rakmen's animal nature.

"We're not going to have a bear problem," said Leah, wearily loading all of their food into the big pack and strapping it closed. "We're being prudent." Jacey's eyes were huge behind her scraggly bangs, and Rakmen saw her slip a chunk of hair into her mouth and start chewing. She edged closer. "Bring the pack," said Leah, grabbing a piece of firewood and a coil of rope.

Jacey slid her hand into his, and they followed Leah to the dark line of forest. About thirty yards from their tents, Leah picked a pine tree with a strong branch about fifteen feet up. She knotted the rope to the chunk of wood, whirled it around her head, and launched it over the branch. The piece of firewood hit the ground at their feet. "We've got to get the pack up as high as we can," said Leah, untying the rope from firewood and retying it around the backpack. "If you lift, I'll pull. One, two, three."

Rakmen hoisted the pack, groaning as every muscle in his body throbbed with pain. Leah pulled on the loose end of the rope.

"Hurry," he grunted.

"Give it one more good push," she said.

He shoved as high as he could. Leah took up the slack in the rope, wrapped it around the trunk of the tree, and secured it with a knot.

"It's a bear piñata," said Jacey, staring up at its lumpy bulk.

"I'm more worried about mice," said Leah.

"It's always the mice," Rakmen blurted. "What is it with the freaking mice?"

"I don't know," Leah sighed, leading them back toward the fire pit, "but I've got to sleep." She and Jacey crawled into their tent.

Rakmen slid into his and sat cross-legged in the middle of it, taking stock. The tent had two doors, one mesh and one nylon. It was too hot to close them both. He zipped the mesh against bugs and then tried to decide about his pants. The last thing he wanted was for a bear to surprise him in his underwear. He started to slide inside the sleeping bag fully clothed, but that was dumb. It wouldn't matter if he were naked or not. The bear would win. Besides, the pants were muddy, bloody, and uncomfortable.

He stripped down to underwear and wadded his pants and sweat-crusted T-shirt in the corner of the tent. The fabric of the sleeping bag was slick against his chest. The murmurs from the other tent subsided, and he listened to water lapping against the rocks, wind in the treetops, and an intermittent skittering of something small moving in the grass.

Out of nowhere, a loon howled wildly. Its cry echoed from the far end of the lake, reminding him how much distance was out there. Lake and forest stretching away and away in every direction. No signs. No bus routes. No easy way home.

He couldn't settle. Every time he dozed off, there were red eyes and piñatas and claws on flesh. He jerked awake in the pitch black. Molly had cuts like that. They'd been downstairs. Group was long over. Crumbs swept. Kids gone. Upstairs, their mothers were deep in conversation. Rakmen sat on the couch flipping through his notebook as Molly put away the last of the art supplies. She tucked a stray doll into the toy trunk and plunked down beside him, her knee resting against his. She leaned forward, elbows on knees, rubbing her eyes. "I'm so empty," she said, breathing lightly and smelling like gingerbread. The closeness of her unnerved him.

"Want me to forage for goldfish crackers in the couch cushions?"

It didn't make her laugh. Instead she slumped back on the couch, leaving her arms limply outstretched, palms up, penitent. That was when he'd seen the thin, parallel scabs on the milky skin of her inner arm.

He absorbed the lines of dried blood and the knowledge of how they got there, slice by careful slice. Without thinking, he'd reached out with one finger to graze her wounds—one, two, three, four. Molly tilted her head until it rested on his shoulder. Her hair spilled over the front of his black hoodie. He breathed her in as she breathed out, and they sat together until they heard the scraping of chairs upstairs.

As he lay in the tent surrounded by night noises and aching in every single part of his body, he thought maybe Molly had been using pain to pour herself back into the empty container of her body. His collection of blisters, bruises, and torn muscles hurt like hell but made him feel present, like his self or soul or whatever filled his limbs from toe to head.

And in spite of how much he ached, Rakmen fell asleep.

CHAPTER 21

When the rising sun turned his tent into a glowing blue cocoon, Rakmen woke and found his limbs still attached. He'd done it. He'd actually survived a night in the woods. He grinned up at the blue nylon until he tried to extricate himself from his sleeping bag.

"Oh crap." He could hardly lift his arms. Wedging himself out of the sleeping bag sent pain shooting through his body. Every single muscle was solid concrete. He rolled over on his knees, wincing as the puffy bruise on his right one touched the ground. Rakmen collapsed onto his stomach, tapping his forehead against the ground in frustration. So he made it through one night. Big deal, sucker. Another day. Another slap in the face.

"I'm not moving," he told the sleeping bag. "Never again." Not for Jacey or Leah or even Molly. "I'm done."

His empty stomach roared. Even his body was against him.

Rakmen cursed under his breath as he pulled on his pants. Everything hurt, but Jacey's oddly comforting pocketful of treasures bumped his thigh, and he checked to make sure the pocket flap was safely buttoned before crawling out of the tent.

Mist, golden from the sun, rose from the flat surface of the lake. The cool morning air brought gooseflesh to his bare chest, but Rakmen could tell the day would be a hot one. Tiny snores came from the orange tent, and he thought he was the first one up until he caught sight of Leah sitting on the rocky point and looking at the lake.

He tensed, trying to read the curved line of her back and the way her arms wrapped around her knees. He approached her like a bomb tech and went into defusing mode. Red wire? Blue wire?

He scuffed his feet to make enough noise not to startle her, and when she looked up, his tension eased a notch. There was a softness to the lines around her eyes that he hadn't seen before. She raised a hand in greeting before turning back to the lake. Rakmen splashed his face in the water, running his fingers through his dark hair.

Jacey woke up and wandered blearily out of the tent, clutching her toothbrush. "Where's the sink?"

Leah actually kind of smiled as she handed Jacey a water bottle. "Spit in the bushes, sweetie."

Rakmen joined Jacey at the bush-sink.

Jacey crossed her eyes at him and let a glop of white bubbles ooze down her chin, zombie-style. They practiced lurching around and foaming at the mouth until Leah told them to pack up their tents.

"Aren't we staying here?" Rakmen asked.

"I want to keep moving."

"Why? This seems okay. No bears."

Her eyes narrowed to slits, making the dark circles under her eyes seem even darker. "I can't stay in one place."

Jacey wiped her mouth on her sleeve and ducked back into her tent. Rakmen could hear her stuffing the sleeping bag into its sack. His own heaviness returned, numbing his limbs like he was an actual zombie.

He deconstructed his tent while Leah made oatmeal. After cleaning up the dishes, they loaded the packs in silence. A loon skimmed to a landing in front of their camp, screaming like a prisoner. When they left that lake behind, Rakmen never wanted to see it again.

After that portage came another lake and another and another. It was almost noon, and even on the water, it was hot. The stifling air buzzed with insects. A particularly irritating deer fly had been harassing Rakmen for ten minutes until it succeeded in a nipping out a chunk of flesh on his ankle. "Damn it!"

"You're naughty," Jacey teased from her spot in the middle of the canoe.

He grimaced.

"There's the next portage," Leah said, pointing ahead to where a wide creek burbled into the lake. "Let's eat before we go."

"Lunch is good," Rakmen said, stomach growling.

While Leah divvied out their rations in neat piles on cloth bandanas, Rakmen and Jacey poked around. The rocky stream bed was fifteen feet wide and less than a foot deep in most places. There were a few deeper holes at the downstream side of the largest boulders. In those spots, the water churned to a white froth.

"Guys," said Leah, calling them back.

Rakmen knew without counting that he had ten crackers stacked neatly beside a pile of nuts, dried apricots, a chunk of cheese, and a one-ounce square of semi-sweet chocolate. The woman couldn't be trusted with plates, but she was precise about crackers.

As they ate, Leah spread out the map between them. "We're here at Wrangel Lake. This portage follows the stream until it gets a little deeper, then there's a short section to paddle and another portage around some rapids."

"How long?" Rakmen asked.

"Two hundred and ten meters followed by a four-fifty."

Rakmen popped the entire piece of chocolate in his mouth and tried not to think about six hundred and sixty meters of fun. If anything, today was worse than yesterday. His blisters had merged into fluid-filled blimps, and his shoulders had been both scraped by his pack straps and bruised by the canoe. He focused on the melty

131

goodness in his mouth and was thankful his tongue didn't hurt.

Leah finished her lunch and walked to the edge of the stream. "The water level seems pretty high this year."

"So?" Rakmen didn't see what that had to do with them.

"We could try to bypass the portage."

Now she had his attention. Anything to avoid carrying that pack and canoe. They changed into sandals, left the packs stowed, and prepared to walk the canoe upstream in the shallow water. It was slow, sloshy going with Leah on one side near the bow, and Rakmen on the other closer to the stern, but it was way easier than portaging. Jacey waded in the water, turning over rocks to look for salamanders.

Branches from maple trees on either side stretched overhead, making a shaded archway. It was cool out of the direct sunlight, and birds flitted everywhere like scraps of chittering confetti. Rakmen saw a little brown and cream-colored one bobbing its tail and poking in the water at the edge of the stream.

"Pssst," he hissed at Jacey to get her attention. "Look."

She stopped flipping rocks to look at the tiny bird wading in inch-deep water like it was in a baby pool. "It's so cute," she said. At the sound of her voice, the bird startled and flew upstream.

"Smooth move," he said, and Jacey hucked a pinecone at him.

"That was a northern waterthrush," said Leah. "Well-spotted."

"You should put it on the list," said Jacey.

"Nuh-uh," said Rakmen. He hadn't agreed to this bird-watching thing.

"Shouldn't all be bad stuff in there." Jacey tipped her head at the pocket that held his notebook. "There's good stuff to write down too."

He glared at her, and Jacey went back to collecting treasures along the bank, taking pictures of the things she couldn't gather. By the time the creek flattened out and was both deep and slow enough for them to paddle upstream, she'd tucked a twisted piece of wood, a gray stone flecked with gold, and a prematurely red maple leaf into the cargo pocket of his pants.

They paddled along the creek for a few hundred feet as it twisted through a grassy meadow. Soon, the terrain turned rocky and sloped upward, and once again the current got fast. They unloaded at the bottom of a narrow chute of white water.

"On the way back, we can run that," said Leah, gesturing to the long run of rapids in an offhand way.

Jacey got excited. "You mean shoot the rapids? That would be epic."

Rakmen immediately started a mental slide show of all the ways that could go wrong. The canoe was made of pieces of wood, which would probably explode into matchsticks on impact with one of those boulders. Fast water would tug at their limbs, and sodden clothes would weigh them down. There was more than one drowned child in that album in the Promise House basement.

Rakmen gulped for air, feeling the pressure to breathe. Dora had suffocated too, not by water in her lungs but by her malformed little heart, which simply could not—no matter how hard it tried—pump enough oxygen to save her.

Instinctively, Rakmen fumbled for his notebook, desperate to pin down the million little things that can lead to death. *Rapids, whitewater, sinking, capsizing.* He saw water, frothing white and churned by hydraulics. He felt the weight of rushing water pinning him to the stream bottom.

"The bird," Jacey said, gripping his sleeve and jerking hard. His pencil skittered across the page, leaving a gray scrawl. "Write down the waterthrush," she insisted. "Say that it wades even though it's smaller than my hand, and to that bird, this stream is like the Grand Canyon or something. Write that."

Blinking away the damp scent of drowning, he wrote *waterthrush, wades and is not swept away.*

"Good," said Jacey. "Thanks." She pulled on her pack and followed her mother up the trail by the stream. Rakmen waited until his breathing slowed. Then he shrugged on his pack, tossed the canoe to his shoulders, and began the steep climb to Pen Lake.

CHAPTER 22

Jacey met Rakmen near the end of the portage. From the claustropho-bic innards of the canoe, he heard her feet on the trail as she doubled back to find him.

"Hey," she said.

He was too focused on the way his load was pounding him into the trail to do anything more than grunt.

"There's a moose," Jacey said, in a breathy, exaggerated whisper, barely able to contain her excitement.

He stopped mid-stride. "Where? Is it close?"

Jacey laughed. "Not here, silly. Out on the lake. Hurry up so you don't miss it."

Hurrying was impossible. Every step hurt from the bruised heel on one foot to the blister on the other, but he plodded after her. There was too much pain radiating through Rakmen's body for him to share her enthusiasm about some overgrown deer.

At the end of the portage, Rakmen unburdened himself as quickly as he could. Filling his lungs and grateful to be able to see again, he scanned the shore of Pen Lake.

Trees, water, and more trees.

"Good one, Jacey. You got me. I totally fell for it."

Jacey held a finger up to her lips and shushed him.

Bewildered, he looked to Leah.

She shrugged and smiled weakly. "Jacey's getting worked up a little prematurely. See that brownish mound down there?" Leah stood next to him and pointed to a grassy bay partway down the lake.

"It looks like a stump."

"Watch."

Moose or no, Rakmen was grateful to stand still. No paddling. No carrying. As long as he didn't move, nothing hurt. Even his mind was quiet in this small, still moment.

Then the stump moved, and Jacey bounced on her tiptoes, tugging on his arm. "Didyousee? Didyousee?"

"Ouch," he said, extracting his arm from her grasp.

The stump was definitely looking at them.

"Let's see if we can sneak up on it and get a closer look," said Leah.

He eyed her while they loaded the canoe, trying to read the set of her shoulders and the lines on her face. He needed to know if she was she leading them someplace they shouldn't go.

"Is this safe?" he asked as they pushed off into the lake.

"Yeah," she said, "and anyway we won't get too close."

Rakmen nodded, and they paddled silently along the shore.

The moose was the biggest animal Rakmen had ever seen outside of a zoo. And the weirdest. Humped back. Gangly legs. Head shaped like a giant peanut. It even had kind of a wattle hanging down from its chin, making it like an insane cross between a turkey, a horse, and a Volkswagen Bug.

Formidable.

That was the word for it. The moose was all bulk and antler and power. Except that it was wading in shallow water and grazing on lily pads, which seemed like a very docile thing to do.

Jacey's paddle slipped and banged the gunnel. She sucked in a startled puff of air as the moose swung its head in their direction, dangling a mouthful of stems and leaves. Rakmen and Leah froze midpaddle-stroke, but the moose didn't care and went back to grazing.

Even without paddling, a slight breeze at their backs kept them moving slowly toward the moose. As they drifted closer, Rakmen could see clouds of flies buzzing around the animal. The moose flicked its ears and spindly tail, swung its head around to brush the biting swarm off its back. The itching of Rakmen's own bug bites redoubled. He scratched one on the back of his neck, and the moose lifted its head, staring right at him.

Its eyes were deep brown and soft, warm in the center but also utterly unfamiliar. The moose had been born here. It knew how to survive. These were its woods, its lakes, its fragrant lilies.

You can be here, it seemed to say.

You can walk and you can carry.

For a while.

Rakmen absorbed every detail of the moose. The ridge of hair on its back. Its velvety muzzle. The jagged edge of a broken bit of antler. He had never been this close to a wild animal.

The moose dipped its head into the water, rooting on the bottom for lilies, and Rakmen realized he'd been holding his breath. He hadn't noticed Jacey pulling out her camera, but the sound of her snapping a picture cut through the air. The moose's head shot up out of the lilies. Jacey took another picture. Something about the tilt of the animal's ears became threatening. A warning.

I hear you, Rakmen thought, reversing his paddle stroke and edging them away. The moose turned and lumbered toward shore, crashing up the bank and disappearing into the forest.

"Wow," Leah breathed.

The three of them grinned at each other, awed and exhilarated.

How brilliant it would be to tell Molly about the moose. Rakmen wanted her to draw it, to capture both the softness and the strength of the creature. He would tell her how it felt to look into its eyes and be invited in.

"Hey, guys," said Leah. "How about camping there?"

They were crossing the mouth of a small bay with a crescent-shaped slice of beach at its end. Up ahead, a high, rocky point stuck out into the lake, and the campsite was on top of it in a grove of pines. They landed at the end of the beach and carried their packs up to the pine-needled grove.

Rakmen walked to the end of the point. To the left, he could see all the way down the lake to the portage they had just crossed. To his right the lake, rippling and dappled with sunlight, opened up. Directly below him, the water was super deep. The bottom was down there somewhere. Probably. Unless it was the portal to Edna's Inuit underworld.

"Think there are piranhas?" said Jacey, coming up behind him and plopping down on the lichen-covered rocks. "Barracuda? Oooh, I know. Sharks!"

"No, stupid. It's a lake. In Canada. Nothing dangerous." But he couldn't shake the uneasy feeling. It bugged him. He was tired of feeling hunted.

"I'm gonna jump," he told Jacey.

Jacey cranked her head up to stare at him. "You're gonna do what?"

"Jump."

Before he could change his mind, Rakmen tore off his T-shirt and unlaced his boots. He was already wearing shorts. He flexed his fingers back, first the left hand, then the right. His knuckles jiffy-popped. Swimming made him think of movies and summer and Grant Pool, where you could see straight to the shark-free bottom.

This was not like swimming.

"So how 'bout it?" he said, "You coming?"

"No way. It's creepy when you can't see what's down there."

Rakmen stood on the edge, staring into the black depths. "Come on," he urged, "there's nothing down there but mud and some sticks."

"I don't swim so good."

"You don't swim?"

She shrugged. "Well, I kinda can."

"Kinda? Like doggy-paddle?" She nodded. No wonder Leah insisted that she wear her life jacket all the time. Rakmen turned back to the drop-off. Somehow knowing Jacey couldn't swim made the distance look farther than it had before.

Buck up and do it, he told himself. He'd survived a night in the wilderness and been up close and personal with a moose. He could jump off a rock. He gripped the rough granite with his toes, flexed his knees, and leapt.

He had time to whoop once, baggy shorts whipping against his thighs, before plunging into the cold, silent water. Engulfed in green, he sank in a cloud of bubbles and stopped motionless in the quiet before swimming for the chrome surface. Nearly out of breath, he burst through, sucking air and wiping the water from his eyes.

"Yes!" he shouted up at Jacey, whose small, worried face poked over the edge of the cliff. "Yes!" he screamed again, pumping one fist before diving back under the water.

CHAPTER 23

By the eighth day on the trail, their odd crew had found a rhythm for their travels. At each portage, Rakmen helped Leah with her pack, which was getting noticeably lighter as they devoured their meals, then he hefted the canoe and headed out with Jacey. She liked being first. As the least encumbered of them, she darted this way and that, catching toads and pointing out birds. Thanks to her, the bird list in his notebook was up to thirty-two species, including a bright blue badass called a kingfisher.

Now that he knew what he was doing, Rakmen set a faster pace than Leah on portages. She plodded along, rarely resting and rarely taking her eyes off the trail. He stuck with Jacey, distracted by her constant commentary, which mostly amused and only sometimes annoyed him.

The day was beautiful. A breeze at their backs cut the heat and sped them along. The first two portages had been easy.

"Alright, people," said Leah, as Rakmen gave a final paddle stroke and maneuvered them into shore, "this is the longest portage of the whole trip."

"How long?" Jacey asked, hefting herself and her pack out of the canoe with practiced skill.

Rakmen rubbed his shoulders. The muscles were tired from the long paddle across Cedar Lake, but it was a well-used, familiar soreness, not salt-in-a-cut excruciating like on the first few days. "Don't ask," he told Jacey, adding to Leah, "Don't tell. That's classified info on a need-to-know basis. I just carry stuff."

Leah grinned at him and gestured Jacey to her side, whispering the distance in her ear. Trail time was working on Leah too. Her tanned face slipped more easily into sweater-soft comfortable, and her silences were easier, as if she carried grief instead of being devoured by it.

"Thanks," she said as Rakmen helped her into her pack. "There should be a couple of canoe rests along the way, but they'll be hard to see while you're carrying. Hey, Jacey," she called, adjusting the tumpline over her forehead, "stay with Rakmen and look for canoe rests, okay?"

Jacey nodded. Rakmen hid his grin. He'd seen the guilty flash on her face as she collected yet another rock. He could hardly believe Leah hadn't noticed his pants pockets bulging like mutant chipmunk cheeks.

"Let's go, girl," he said, throwing up the canoe in one smooth motion.

The trail sloped upward on an exposed granite ridge. A few stunted trees had managed to worm their roots into soil-filled cracks, but it was mostly open. The midday sun radiated off the rocks, turning the inside of the canoe into a mini-sauna. By the time the trail moved into a more heavily forested section, sweat had soaked Rakmen's shirt. Jacey's chubby calves, which were all he could see from under the canoe, had gone from bouncy skips to a dragging shuffle.

"So how long is it?" he asked.

Jacey stopped mid-trail. "You told me not to tell you."

"Keep moving," he grunted, "and tell me. I wanna know now."

"Nineteen hundred and something," she said, turning about-face and marching on.

Kind of useless information, he realized. The pain in his shoulders determined whether a portage was long or short. This one was

140

definitely long. "See if you can find a place to take a break."

"Lazy," she giggled, darting out in front of him.

"Jacey—" he roared, which only made her laugh harder.

Birdsong rang out from close by on his left. The melody rose, half-bell, half burbling spring, a clean and promising sound. Far off and to the right, another bird of the same kind answered, and their conversation carried Rakmen around another bend in the trail. Too bad Leah wasn't close enough to ID it for him.

"There's a canoe rest up here," Jacey called.

"You're a lifesaver," said Rakmen, catching up with her. "Direct me."

"See that big spruce and this smaller one here?" Jacey said, patting a trunk. "They're the supports." Leah's natural history lessons had begun to stick. Both Rakmen and Jacey could name the trees and many of the smaller plants that filled the forest floor.

Rakmen positioned himself in front of the two spruces, tipped the bow up, and rested the stern on the ground. Now he could see the rough-cut log nailed crosswise between the trees about six feet off the ground. He lifted the stern a few inches and edged forward until he could rest the bow on the crossbar. Once it felt balanced, he set the stern down with a gentle thud and scrambled out from under the canoe.

Jacey had already flipped off her pack and pulled out a water bottle. Tendrils of hair clung to her sweaty cheeks. She slapped at a stray mosquito and handed him the water. "Are we almost there?"

He shrugged. "Can you dig up some chocolate?"

Jacey squinted at him. "You mean raid the lunch?"

"You bet."

Looking guilty but happy, she tore into the carefully rationed lunch bag. After this long on the trail, Rakmen saw the logic of Leah's maniacal packing. There'd been method to her madness of carefully measured scoops of dried fruit and the way she'd counted crackers like the three of them were parrots on a diet. Lunch was efficiently-packed, high-protein fuel, exactly the right amount for each of them. No waste. No excess to carry.

Rakmen unwrapped the white paper from his precious chunk of chocolate.

"She's gonna be mad," Jacey warned.

"She won't know if you divvy out the lunch."

That was enough convincing for Jacey to chomp down on hers with her oversized front teeth. "Look," she said, flashing her chocolate-smeared teeth at him in a big grin and holding out the candy, "a beaver ate my chocolate."

Sure enough, her bite mark reminded him of the gnawed beaver sticks she'd been collecting by the armload. Leah made her leave most of them behind in the interest of weight, but Jacey was determined to find the perfect one. Ten of the top contenders were strapped to the side of her pack. From the back, she looked like a well-armed dwarf.

Rakmen rolled his shoulders and stretched. He was getting stronger every day. He liked the increased definition of his muscles and the way he had grown into the demands of the trail. He liked the simplicity of his daily tasks. Carry the canoe. Paddle. Pitch the tents. Purify water. Light a fire. By now, he knew how to do these things as well as Leah. He possessed something of what he had sensed in the canoeist they had seen from Edna's dock. Rakmen tucked that feeling into his pocket along with Jacey's treasures.

The sound of panting on the trail sent Jacey into a frantic stashing of the lunch. Leah rounded the bend in the trail, oblivious to their subterfuge. "Hey Mom, there's a rock over here where you can rest." Jacey bounced back and forth on the balls of her feet, licking her lips to remove telltale signs of thievery.

Leah backed up toward the rock like a truck to a loading dock. Rakmen fought the urge to make back-up beeps. Leah didn't usually want to take the pack all the way off because it was so hard to get back on, which meant she had to find a place to rest the behemoth and take the weight off her shoulders, but she also had to be able to stand up again. There was nothing worse than turning turtle, she'd assured them one night around the campfire. When she acted out falling over in her pack, he'd laughed until his sides hurt.

"Water," she panted, and Jacey raced over with the bottle. After a long gulp, she asked, "How come you're so perky? Portage isn't long enough for you?"

Jacey flashed Rakmen her best spy look. "Nah, we've been resting. Look how cool this spot is."

It was, Rakmen had to admit, seriously cool.

On one side of the trail, tightly-packed spruce grew right up to the rocky path, but on the other side, the land sloped down gently into a wide, circular meadow ringed with other kinds of trees. He could pick out yellow birch and sugar maple. Tall grasses rippled in the breeze like green waves. Hundreds of dragonflies zipped and hovered. It was, Rakmen thought, the kind of place where long-lost lovers ran slow-mo into each other's arms, or vampires got all sparkly and made out.

"I can't look," Leah groaned. "It makes me want to take a nap." She hefted herself up from the boulder. "I'm gonna keep going. You two stick together." She stared hard at Rakmen, reinforcing the command.

"I don't go anywhere without her," he said and then raised a hand to his mouth and pretended to whisper, "because she won't let me."

Jacey elbowed him. "You'd be lost without me."

"Don't be long," Leah warned and started off down the trail.

As soon as she was out of sight, Rakmen and Jacey finished their chocolates.

"You about ready?" he asked.

"Can't we explore a little?"

He looked at the canoe and then down the trail after Leah. "Five minutes."

She squealed happily, grabbed his hand, and dragged him into the sunshine.

He hadn't really intended to go off on one of her expeditions, but with chocolate coursing through his veins and the sun soaking into his face and arms, he went easily. *Au large* was beginning to sink into his bones. Maybe you didn't need to know where you were going or spend too much time thinking about where you'd been. You only needed to move forward. In the last few days, he'd hardly thought about home and whether his parents were managing to patch things together. Interspersed in his notebook with sing-song bird names like *cedar waxwing, merganser,* and *pine warbler* were *blister on heel, broken flashlight,* and *too little chocolate.* Small complaints.

Rakmen turned his face to the sun. The light through his closed lids was deep orange. The air around him burbled and buzzed, warbled and whined. On every side, creatures were moving and rustling, living and dying. For the merest pause between heartbeats, it seemed to be alright that living and dying were all tangled up together. Dora was with him in her own kind of aching way.

A sudden, high-pitched wail sent panic jolting through him.

His eyes snapped open. Jacey was crumpled in the grass, her face twisted in pain. He raced toward her, a thousand terrible possibilities flickering against his vision.

He hadn't been watching.

He'd promised to watch.

"What's wrong?" he panted, wrapping his arms around her. Any second her chest could stop moving, her eyes would go blank, and—

Jacey leaned into him, moaning. "I stubbed my toe."

"Your toe?" His fear uncoiled then reformed into a hot, angry ball in his stomach. He pushed her away.

She tumbled off his lap and burst into tears.

Rakmen pressed his hands over his ears.

"I'm hurt," she wailed.

"Shut up."

She cried harder. "You're supposed to take care of me."

"You're not my sister," he snarled.

Jacey curled away from him, her back shaking with sobs. His anger drained away as quickly as it had come. His stomach turned sour. She looked so tiny balled up in the grass, so fragile in a great big world. He couldn't stand himself.

He made the world ugly by standing in it.

Dora had deserved better.

So did Jacey.

For days, the trapped feeling had been absent. Now it loomed over him again, threatening to crush the air from his lungs. He shouldn't be here making everyone else's life worse than it already was. But he was stuck on this portage, in the middle of nowhere, in his own broken life.

A large dragonfly buzzed him. Another landed on his arm, twisting its huge triangular head one way and then the other. Its wings trembled slightly. The tiny claws at the end of its legs scratched Rakmen's skin. To the mosquitos in this meadow, it was a heavily-armored attack helicopter, and yet Rakmen could crush it with one hand.

He crouched beside Jacey and touched her back, "I'm sorry."

She pushed herself to a sitting position, gulping back tears. "It's okay," she said in a tiny voice, avoiding his eyes.

"No, it's not." Rakmen rubbed his neck. He brushed her bangs out of her face and wiped her tears. "How's your toe? Do we need to amputate?"

She laughed at that and tackled him. They went sprawling in the grass, and Rakmen's elbow smacked against something hard. It was his turn to cry out. They stopped wrestling and felt their way through the grass. Rakmen saw a dark ridge half buried in grass and dirt. "This must be what you stubbed your toe on." When he touched it, orange rust came off on his fingertips. "It's metal. How weird is that?" Rakmen scraped at the dirt around the object. Jacey crawled forward to see what he had found.

"Let's dig it out," he suggested.

Jacey was already up, stubbed toe and all, running toward her pack. "I'll get some of my beaver sticks," she called over her shoulder.

Rakmen rocked back on his heels. The meadow was a circular depression in a sea of dense forest. From the air, it would be a mere blip of pale green. He couldn't imagine how such a large piece of metal could have ended up so far into the wilderness.

Jacey returned, panting and waving two beaver sticks in eye-puncturing gyrations.

"Hold your weapons."

She saluted and delivered a stick. When they were both

well-armed, he gave the command to dig. Soon a U-shaped piece of metal protruded from the soil. Jacey flailed along one side of it, sending dirt flying behind her like a dog, while he excavated the other side. Soon, Rakmen could make out a strip of metal eighteen inches long and two inches wide and bent nearly double. Looking closer, he realized that the strip was actually two parts with zig-zagging edges that fit together like interlocking teeth.

"Halt, soldier," he said, stilling Jacey's stick with one hand. Years of corrosion had smoothed the sharp edges the device once had, but something about it made Rakmen queasy. "Let's take her easy."

Jacey squatted beside him, twitching with excitement. Rakmen poked away the dirt in the center of the bent metal. A few inches down he hit a flat, metal circle connected to the ends of the U by thin strips. Expanding the trench in both directions, he found a metal loop welded to one end of the U and, attached to that, a rusty length of chain link.

Rakmen dug his fingers under the chain and pulled. The earth around the artifact cracked, the stems of the grass breaking and bending as if some animal were digging up from below. He strained against the roots that were twisted in the bent bits of the metal object. Jacey grabbed him around the waist and squeezed.

He dropped the chain and twisted toward her. "What's wrong?"

"I'm helping," she said, tightening her grip and burrowing her face in his side.

He'd been about to peel her away, but instead he put his arm around her. "I'm really sorry about earlier."

"I know." Her voice was muffled against his shirt.

"Do you want me to get this thing out?"

She nodded, still clinging to him.

"I'll puke up my chocolate if you keep squeezing me. Give me some room to work."

She backed off a few feet, red-faced. Rakmen tousled her hair and then wrapped his hands around the chain again. Layers of rust flaked off in his hands, and the peaty smell of dislodged earth filled his nose. With a final heave, the device pulled free.

"What is it?" Jacey asked, leaning in close.

Recognition jiggled in the back of his mind. The circular plate, the metal teeth . . . memories of a sixth-grade field trip to an Oregon Trail historic site flooded back. "It's a trap."

"Like a booby trap?"

"No, an animal trap. See how this part can open like alligator jaws?"

Jacey's eyes grew huge. "It's a good thing we used sticks. What if our hands got chomped?"

"It's been tripped," he said. "Been here a long time too."

"I want it," Jacey announced.

Rakmen rubbed his sweaty forehead. Of course, Jacey wanted it. The biggest treasure in her collection. "Your mom will never go for that."

"Mom!" Jacey gasped.

"Oh man." Rakmen knew they'd been at their archeological site far more than five minutes. Leah was probably freaking out. He reached for Jacey's hand. "Let's go." She wiggled out of his grasp and picked up the trap, cradling it in her arms like a baby as she speed-walked back to her pack.

"You're not seriously thinking about carrying that, are you? We've still got a long way to portage." She clutched it tighter and lower-lipped him.

There wasn't time to fight with her. Not if they wanted to catch up with Leah before she totally lost her shit. "Let me hold it while you put on your pack."

He got Jacey situated and pointed her down the trail, wishing that the rusty smears all over her shirt looked less like blood. Before he picked up the canoe, Rakmen took a last look around the meadow.

Someone had set the trap a very long time ago. Set it and left it or lost it or forgot. A whisper of the long-dead trapper and his quarry rustled through the tall grass. Rakmen shivered. He lifted the canoe and followed Jacey. He did not want to stay here any longer.

CHAPTER 24

Rakmen's anxiety rose as he neared the end of the portage. His legs were crumbling with exhaustion. He hadn't stopped again to rest because he expected trouble. Leah had probably come unglued when they hadn't shown up on time.

He cursed the stupid-long portage.

And himself for wasting time in the meadow.

A small bird with a striped head and white throat flitted across the trail in front of him and perched on a fallen log. Rakmen named it without thinking. *White-throated sparrow.* The bird's throat pulsed in and out as it belted out a rising, repetitive song. It was so very alive and yet so delicate—like the organ that every second sent blood pulsing through his own body. They were always so close to the knife-edge. A million things could still the heart.

At the end of the portage, he listened for the sound of crying and heard only the water lapping against the shore. When he set the canoe down and could finally see, Jacey was pulling off her boots and socks, and Leah was examining the trap.

"This is a pretty amazing find," she said, smiling up at him.

He nodded, scanning her expression for trouble under the surface. Nothing. He eased the pack off his back and sat down by Jacey.

"How come she's not mad?" he whispered.

"I didn't tell her you pushed me."

"I said I was sorry."

She waved her stinky socks in his face. "Smell my foot wrath!"

Rakmen warded her off with the sign of the cross. Once she'd splashed off to look for frogs, he sat down beside Leah for a closer look at the trap. He ran a finger along its teeth. "What was it for?"

"Beaver," she said. "The French trappers did a bang-up trade in the early days, and it's too small for bear."

"How old is it?"

She wrinkled her forehead. "Over a hundred years probably. I'm trying to remember when the settlement on this lake was active."

Rakmen was surprised all over again. "People actually lived here?"

"Some. Not many. The winters are brutal." Leah unfolded the map on her knees. "We're right here on Allard Lake. The remains of an old farm are here." She pointed to a spot on the map opposite the portage. Across the water, Rakmen could see a wide grassy clearing.

"Is there anything left?" he asked.

"I think so. Foundations of a farmhouse. A few old timbers."

"Can we check it out?"

"Sure." They checked the map again and located a campsite near one end of the meadow. "Why don't we set up camp and then walk over? That last portage wiped me out," Leah suggested.

"What's this mean?" Rakmen asked, poking at a small square with a number four in it printed in the middle of the lake.

"Four days from here to anywhere else," said Leah, getting stiffly to her feet. "Come on, Jacey," she called, "we're ready to roll."

Rakmen stared at the number four. The map highlighted canoe routes in yellow, and he could see that this lake was a kind of hub. Several different routes passed through it. Backtracking with his finger along the last portage, Rakmen traced their own route from campsite to campsite until he poked one finger at the black square indicating Uncle Leroy's ramshackle cabin.

It had taken them eight days to get where they were, but they'd taken a circuitous route and had been slow at first. If they had bypassed the Petra River and had taken a portage around several lakes, they could've made it here in four days. There was another route, also estimated at four days' travel time, that led north to a ranger station on Lake Lavielle. A third led to a small community on the western edge of the wilderness area called Branvin, where their food resupply box was waiting for them.

He folded the map and placed it back in the waterproof bag.

Leah pointed out a bird called a white-breasted nuthatch.

"Write it down," said Jacey, nudging him.

"Yes, ma'am. That puts us at thirty-three species."

"Thirty-four," said Leah, pointing at a bird skimming over the treetops. "Merlin."

"Like the wizard?" Jacey asked.

"It's a falcon."

Leah gave a mini-lecture on its birdy attributes.

Rakmen added *merlin* to his notebook, scribbling underneath *super fast, predator, eats songbirds*. The sparrow he'd seen on the trail would be toast if that guy got his claws into it.

They saw the merlin again as they paddled across Allard Lake, soaring and swooping like a fighter jet. Death from above—if you were a bird.

They set up camp quickly, following the routine that had developed over the intervening days. Rakmen unloaded the packs while Leah collected wood. Jacey found the food pouches for the evening meal, and then he helped her set up the tents. It was clockwork now.

In forty-five minutes, they were hiking to the old homestead. Without the canoe weighing him down, Rakmen was light on his feet. It made him want to try out for track next season.

Jacey led the way along the shoreline, collecting fluffy, white seed pods from the tall grass.

"Whatchya want those for?" he asked.

"Duh! Pillows."

He smiled at her. For the past few days, she'd been making fairy houses out of bark and moss. Of course they needed pillows. He plucked another handful for her as he walked.

A little farther on, Jacey stopped again. "What are those?" she asked.

Under the water were two obviously man-made structures, mostly crumbled and rotting away, but their form still discernible.

Intact, each one would have been about five feet across in both directions, an open box made of squared-off timbers and filled with bowling-ball sized rocks. One was about four feet from shore. The other farther out.

"Those are the old cribs," said Leah.

Jacey squinted at her. "Like baby cribs?"

The word *baby* sent alarm bells ringing in Rakmen's head. His every instinct was to divert attention from that unstable ground. "It's like *MTV Cribs*," he said. "You know, houses."

"Houses for what?"

"They weren't houses," said Leah as if she hadn't noticed the word *baby* at all. "The old timers used cribs to hold up the decking of their docks."

She headed away from the water, and they wandered after her. Jacey found the crumbled remains of a stone chimney and what was left of an ancient wood stove with grass and wildflowers growing up through its many cracks. Other than that and a rectangular depression in the ground marking the floor plan of the one-room cabin, nothing was left.

"I wonder what it was like to live here," he said.

"Pretty lonely, I expect," said Leah, "so far from anyone else."

"I'm not lonely out here with you guys," Jacey piped in.

"Maybe not now," Leah replied, "but you'd get sick of us eventually."

Rakmen paced out the impression of the four walls. It was a tiny space to spend the winter. He tried to imagine being cooped up with the wind whistling through cracks in the logs and snow, snow, snow in every direction.

He retraced his steps from the old homestead to the ruins of the dock. Someone else had walked exactly where he placed his feet.

Other eyes had stared out at this same lake, day in and day out, for years, maybe decades. Out there, in the rest of the world, in his old life, everything was different—cell phones and tablet computers, self-parking cars and internet glasses—but here . . .

Rakmen turned quickly, half-expecting to see smoke curling above the sod roof of the little square building, and the trapper saying good-bye to his family as he went to check his traplines. What he actually saw was Jacey on a little hillock at the far side of the meadow, waving wildly.

"Come here," she hollered. "You've got to see this!"

Leah shrugged at him. "More fairies?"

His laughter came easily, rolling up from the bottom of his stomach. He strode toward Jacey, shaking his head. The girl was a goofball. Rakmen's good humor lasted until he reached Jacey, where it trickled out like a last breath.

She was standing beside a short iron fence that enclosed four graves all in a row. The stone markers were soft-edged from years of weather, and orange lichen clung to the surface, but the rough-etched names remained.

Joseph Allard, mon aîné
Marie Allard, ma troisième-née
Jean Baptiste Allard, mon sixième-né
Thérèse Allard, née Vallée, ma jolie femme,
  et notre dernière née, Adèle

"What does it say?" Jacey asked, clasping and unclasping her hands.

Leah swayed on her feet, the blood draining from her face. "The first three were children. The first born, the third, and the sixth. The mother was buried with a baby." She stepped backward unsteadily and slumped to the ground. Jacey burrowed under her mom's arm until she was practically in Leah's lap.

Rakmen could not tear his eyes from the graves. The air in his lungs seemed more like oil than oxygen. He tried to catch his breath, fighting the suffocating heat and the rising buzz of insects around them.

"Why did so many of them die?" Jacey whispered.

Leah pulled Jacey closer. "Oh honey, in the old days, kids died all the time." Her voice fluttered like a tattered sheet. "No medicine. No hospitals. People got sick and . . . It happened all the time . . ."

Rakmen imagined the trapper shoveling earth onto his wife's vacant face. The remaining children—the second, the fourth, and the fifth—would be afraid of the way tears streamed into their father's beard. Dazed by loss, they'd stumble into one another in the small cabin, wrapping bundles of food and rolling blankets, preparing to abandon this cursed place.

Their ghosts thundered over him.

"We need to go," he said, urging Leah and Jacey to their feet. They were four days from anywhere and way too close to the dead.

CHAPTER 25

Rakmen dropped another armload of wood by the fire pit.

"You can stop," Leah said, feeding another stick to the flames.

The light was fading. Soon it would be too dark to see the downed maple he was systematically dismembering into firewood. The trapper's family had stayed with Rakmen all afternoon, their ghosts grasping at his heels. He couldn't beat them away, but he could keep moving.

His right arm was sore from sawing. His head pounded, and the world was distant. Once, the maniac cry of a woodpecker penetrated the shroud, but Rakmen bore down harder on the dry wood, sending shavings into the air and imagining the trapper skinning beaver in bloody strips. The man was gone. Rakmen did not know him. Yet what the man felt as he had buried his family, Rakmen felt now. He did not like the way it pierced him.

Jacey had fallen asleep early, leaving him beside the fire with Leah. She'd been steadily feeding it wood but hadn't made a dent in his supply. Rakmen had cut enough for an army to overwinter, and it still wasn't enough.

Up until they'd found the graves, Rakmen had been in the rhythm of *au large*. It was immediate, without memory most of the time. At the homestead, he'd stumbled into someone else's life, and Dora had come back on the ragged coattails of the trapper's children.

No matter how much wood he cut, he could not dislodge the memories. They were tearing him limb from limb. The sky darkened, becoming an upside-down bowl of stars cupped over the pulsating bed of coals. When it was too dark to cut any more wood, he sat across the fire from Leah, too keyed up to sleep. Rakmen watched her through the distorted column of heated air that rose from the bed of coals.

"Do you think they left?" he asked.

She stirred the embers of the fire with a charred stick. "Who?"

"The trapper and the kids who lived. Do you think they left this place? Is that why the trap got left behind?"

Leah toe-nudged the rusty beaver trap at her feet, considering. "The trap could have been dragged somewhere he couldn't find it."

"By a trapped beaver?"

She shrugged and poked at the coals again.

He didn't want to think about an animal caught in those metal teeth, thrashing into deeper water, trailing blood. He did not want to think about that at all.

"But you're asking if I think he left after his wife died," she said. "I doubt it. Those French Canadians were made of tougher stuff than I."

In the dim orange light, her lips quirked up in a small, sad smile. He studied her, seeing all the pieces of her, all at once. She was his teacher and his mother's friend. Jacey's mom and the dead baby's too. She was a woman who broke plates and cried at Promise House. She had dragged them out here kicking and screaming. Yet on the trail, she seemed to be finding a way to put herself back together.

"I think you're tough," he said.

Her eyes flicked up from the coals. "You do?"

"Yeah, but there's one thing I don't get."

Leah threw another log on the fire. "What's that?"

"Molly's mom won't let her do anything. No sleepovers with friends. No driving. No dates."

"Kate is scared she'll lose her too," said Leah.

"I know," said Rakmen, "but are you not? I mean, you brought us out here where anything could happen." She stiffened. "I'm not criticizing," he explained. "I was wondering. Aren't you afraid?"

On the water, a loon howled. The sound had grown so familiar that it no longer sent adrenaline coursing through Rakmen. Instead he listened for a reply, and soon enough it came, muted and distant, from some neighboring lake.

Leah zipped her fleece jacket against the growing chill of the night. "I came because this place—these trees, the lakes, the trails—they don't care if I'm happy or miserable. They take me the way I am."

Rakmen rubbed the calluses on his left palm with his thumb, nodding. He got that. He was a tiny dot on the map of the world. Under this sky and in these woods, it didn't matter that he had failed as a brother. Somehow that made Dora easier to face.

"Mrs. Tatlas," he asked, suddenly unable to use her first name. "What happened to your baby?"

She dropped the stick on the coals where it caught and flamed, deepening the shadows of her face.

"I'm sorry," he said. "I shouldn't have asked."

"No, it's okay," she said, taking a deep breath. "When your baby dies like he did, most people pretend he never existed. That's worse than asking." She picked up another stick from Rakmen's wood pile and stirred the coals. A puff of sparks floated into the night, winking out above their heads. "He was stillborn."

"Jacey told me that," said Rakmen. "I was wondering why."

Leah rocked back and forth on the log bench. "I remember thinking when I was pregnant that I wouldn't have to start worrying about him until he was born. I didn't know he could die like that. So fast."

Rakmen could feel the gentle weight of Dora in his arms, hear her snuffling, smell her milk-scented breath. He'd wanted to get her to sleep quickly so he could go out with Juan. She was holding him up, alternately crying and panting. He'd hummed distractedly, not really noticing the way her breathing changed, becoming wheezy and shallow.

"Jordan was past his due date. The doctor kept wanting to induce labor. I kept saying no, everything's fine."

Dora's breath came in frantic gulps. Her eyes wheeled, terrified by the way her inner machinery was breaking down, but she was a baby and didn't know what was happening. And he was slow, too stupid slow, to realize what was happening.

"But the placenta started to tear off."

As a gray tinge snuck into Dora's cheeks, Rakmen had screamed for help. He'd pressed two fingers to her sternum—again, again, again. He'd covered her tiny nose and soft lips with his own mouth, desperate to send his own life into her lungs—again, again, again.

"By the time we were at the hospital, it was too late."

Dad wrenched Dora from his arms, but by then, her eyes had dimmed and gone.

Across the dying fire, Leah's shoulders trembled, and the wet tracks on her cheeks gleamed. Rakmen's heart was flailing against the bone cage of his chest, thrashing its way to deeper water.

"I'm sorry," he said. "I'm so sorry."

She poured water over the coals. A hissing, choking cloud of steam rose in a gray column. "Let's get some sleep. I want to move early tomorrow."

CHAPTER 26

"You can't take it."

"Mom!" The drawn-out whine of Jacey's protest woke Rakmen from a nightmare. In the dream, they were back on Pen Lake where they'd seen the moose. He'd jumped off the high rocks like he had in real life, but he'd gone too deep to make it to the surface again. He thrashed out of his sleeping bag, panting.

"I'll carry it."

"It weighs too much."

"But—"

"The trap stays."

Rakmen waited until the argument was over and the frantic pounding in his chest had calmed before pulling on his pants and climbing out of his tent. Jacey sulked over oatmeal while Leah finished rolling their sleeping pads.

He glanced at his watch. It wasn't even seven o'clock.

Bleary-eyed, Rakmen headed to the lake to dip his head. Fog hung over the water, concealing the homestead across the bay, but the graves were there, the bones churned each year through freeze and thaw.

Dora was buried in a cemetery high on the hills over Portland. For the funeral, their procession of cars had followed the hearse up a steep, twisting road. Queasy waves of nausea had swept over him, intensified by the cloying perfume his mother had worn. He'd gulped back bile, each swallow a struggle against the knotted tie and stiff collar.

Rakmen dried his face on the bottom of his T-shirt. The cold, wet fabric against his stomach sent a shiver through him. He returned to the fire, where Jacey stared mournfully at the beaver trap.

She flashed puppy eyes at him. "Can you take it?"

"Sorry, girl. My pockets are full."

She returned to full sulk, gnawing on a piece of hair. Her brother's bones were ash in a box in his crib. Rakmen squatted beside her. "You can take some pictures, you know."

"It's not the same."

"I know, but it's still cool. Nobody back home knows what a beaver trap looks like. Set it up on that rock for a fashion shoot." That won a smile, and Jacey scurried to the task while he and Leah broke camp. For once, he was as eager to move on as she was.

Thirty minutes later they were skimming through the rising mist toward the first portage of the day. It was a long one—five hundred and thirty meters—and the landing spot was a jumble of rocks. He'd have to be careful not to ding up his canoe.

Uncle Leroy's canoe.

But Rakmen couldn't help feeling possessive. He was the one who had carried it for the past nine days. He had propelled it mile after painful mile with his aching limbs. The blond wood reminded him of Molly and the way sailors always call their ships she.

"You can stop paddling," he told Leah and Jacey. "I'll ease us in."

They rested their paddles across their knees while he slowed the canoe and deftly brought the bow into a narrow slot between two rocks. Once their gear was piled on the rocky shore, Leah helped him lift the canoe out of the water and rest it on a semi-flat spot, then the three of them stood together looking up the path. If you could call it a path. From the shoreline, the bank was more rock than soil and sloped up steeply. He'd have to pick his way like a mountain goat for at least fifty feet.

"Are you going to be able to manage it?" Leah asked. "The balance will be tricky."

She was right. On flat ground, the canoe balanced perfectly on his shoulders, but here he'd have to tilt it to match the angle of the slope. The weight would try to pull him backward.

"I think I'll take my pack up the steep part first. Or I can take yours and you can take the smaller one up."

"I've got it," she said.

He nodded, shouldered his pack and took Jacey's pack in his other hand. "Let's go, girl. You first." Jacey began to scramble up the rocks, pointing out good handholds along the way. He kept close behind her in case she slipped. At the top, they high-fived. "Wait here until I come back with the canoe."

"I wanna go," she said, scuffing her boots in the dirt.

He frowned at her, the uneasiness he'd felt earlier returning. "Take some pictures. I think we should stick together on this one."

On the way back down, he skidded on some loose pebbles and slid a few feet before catching himself. He frowned as he dabbed at the scrape on his palm.

"Do you need a Band-Aid?" Leah asked when she saw fresh blood on his shirt.

"Nah. Let's get out of here." This lake was bad news all around.

He hefted Leah's pack so she could slide into the straps. As she adjusted the tumpline on her forehead, Rakmen knelt and re-tied his boots, knotting them extra tight. Once the canoe was up, he couldn't afford to catch a lace.

Rakmen scanned the lake one last time. The fog had lifted, and the meadow where the trapper's family had lived was a pale green smudge along the far shore. It was sunny, but a wind was rising, bringing with it a warning of trouble like a far-off siren. He turned back to the steep slope. For once, Jacey had listened. She waited at the top, taking pictures of tree bark or something. Leah was halfway up, bent almost double under the weight of her back and picking her way through the rocks. Twenty more feet and she'd be out of the tough part.

Thin clouds streaked by. The upper air was moving fast. Rakmen bent toward the canoe, gripping the thwart inside the gunnels. A gust of wind flattened his T-shirt against his body and filled his mouth with a metallic tang. Waves splattered against the rocks around him. He was tensing for the swift movement needed to bring the craft overhead when he heard a quick, throaty gasp. The surprised intake of breath was barely audible over the wind and waves but somehow more piercing than any alarm.

After the gasp came a *pop* like the release of a jar lid.

A tight, artificial sound. The rupture of some sealed chamber, cracked wide open.

And then Leah fell.

She thudded down the rocky slope.

Jacey screamed and was still screaming when Leah's body slammed into the ground at his feet. She was face up, her shoulders wrenched back by the straps of the pack. Her pupils were black tubes connected straight to her animal brain. The wind knocked out of her came back in a wheeze that racked through her body.

Rakmen dropped to his knees, loosening the buckles on the straps so Leah was no longer pinioned.

"It's bad," she said, the words cracking against each other. "Broken."

"No," he said, unwilling to agree.

"Look."

Her foot bent inward at an unnatural angle like the head of a dead chicken. Fear screamed through him. Jacey clattered down beside them in an avalanche of pebbles as Rakmen slid his hands under Leah's back, lifted her off the pack and laid her on the ground. Leah's face contorted with pain then relaxed as she lost consciousness.

"Don't die," Jacey shrieked, throwing herself toward Leah.

Rakmen caught Jacey around the waist and pulled her into his arms. She pounded her fists against Rakmen's chest. "Don't let her die!"

The ground listed beneath Rakmen as if the ever-increasing wind had brought swells to the earth. His thoughts trampled each other.

They needed help.

There was no one.

Not 911.

Not his father.

Not Edna.

"Do something!" Jacey screamed. "You can fix her."

Four days from anywhere.

The only someone was him.

Rakmen shook Jacey, forcing her to sit down next to the canoe. "Shut up! I need to think." Jacey glued her mouth into a tight little line. Rakmen palmed his hand toward the ground—stay. She dipped her chin and stayed. He crawled to Leah. All he could see was glassy white between her slitted lids. Beneath the skin, her eyeballs twitched. Her breath came in shallow rasps. Rakmen raked his hands through his hair, pulling hard. If only his dad were here, he'd know what to do.

He had to focus.

He needed to know how bad the break was. Compound fractures were the worst, his dad always said. Infection was the enemy. He crawled to the lower half of Leah's body, flexing his fingers. Right in front of him was Leah's scuffed, dirt-covered boot. The weight of it pulled against the foot inside.

Sweat dribbled down the side of his face, only to be sucked away by the wind. He shivered. "I've got to get the boot off," he said, trying to sound like his dad, "and quickly, before she wakes up. It'll hurt less that way."

"What if you make it worse?" Jacey asked.

He wiped his forehead with the back of his forearm. "We've got to know how bad it is. Besides, her foot will swell in the boot. Come over here. I need you to hold her steady."

Jacey crouched beside him and cradled Leah's leg in her hands. Shaking, Rakmen picked at the double-knotted laces until they were as loose as possible.

He paused, unsure of what to do next.

The boot was still tight around the bones of her ankle. He didn't know where it was broken or how badly or what damage he could do removing the boot, but Leah moaned, and he knew he couldn't wait. He wasn't sure he could do this if she were awake and in pain.

"Hold her calf as steady as you can," he said. "I'm going to ease the boot off."

Jacey blinked back tears and shifted position. "Now?"

Rakmen held the heel with one hand and the toe in the other. "Now," he said and pulled.

With a wet, gristly sound, the boot came off. Afraid to stop what he had started, Rakmen peeled off Leah's sock as well. Purple bloomed under the skin, spreading as he watched. The dents left by her sock were already being erased by swelling. Lumps where he didn't think there should be lumps protruded, but the skin hadn't split.

He supported the foot with Jacey's fleece jacket and sent her to dampen a bandana from the lunch pack. Wiping the cool cloth over Leah's face, he worked to rouse her, trying all the while not to see, superimposed on Leah's immobile face, his sister's and the way her lips had gone blue-black at the end.

"Come on. Wake up," he pleaded. When her eyes flickered open, he nearly wept. "You're alright."

She blinked slowly. "I don't think so, Rakmen."

"You'll be okay," he stammered. "We'll get out of here."

She shook her head very slowly. "I can't walk."

Buzzing filled Rakmen's ears and head and limbs. This wasn't right. Things had finally started coming together. A few good days. That's what they'd had. Now everything was broken again. His arm lifted of its own volition, the fingers curling into a fist. Sick churning filled him. He wanted to break and pound and destroy. He pulled his fist back, his muscles tensed, fury obscuring his vision.

He should've known better.

He pounded his fist into the ground beside him.

Over and over, he hit the ground. Blind to the way Leah feebly struggled to stop him. Deaf to Jacey's hysterical sobs.

Raging, guttural sounds burst from his throat.

What was supposed to happen was this—

The adult in the room knows what to do. Babies don't die. Boys don't bash their fists bloody against the ground.

Finally, Jacey's wails pierced the hot, enveloping rage.

Leah's eyelids fluttered, and her hand fell away from where it clutched the side of his shirt. Panic filled his lungs until it felt like the dream, like drowning.

Out on the lake, a loon wailed. A warning.

A command.

Rakmen pressed his palms flat against the dirt.

He ignored the churning in his stomach and breathed deeply, catching the scent of pine and wet earth. Rain was coming, they were four days from anywhere, and he was the only one capable of doing anything.

CHAPTER 27

Rakmen helped Jacey to her feet. She was trembling. Rakmen's insides were jelly, but he smudged her tears away with his thumb. "It's gonna rain."

She nodded.

"We can't camp here. It's too rocky."

Jacey nodded again.

"I need you to hold the canoe while I load it and help your mom in, okay?"

Her eyes filled with tears again, but she bit her lip and dipped her chin one more time.

"That's my girl."

Rakmen slid the canoe into the water, and Jacey crouched beside the bow. He returned to Leah and felt her pulse like he'd seen his dad do when someone got injured. It tapped a steady rhythm against his fingertips. That was good. It reassured him.

He nudged her shoulder gently, and Leah's eyes opened. "Are you in a lot of pain?" he asked. Her eyes darted to where Jacey waited by the canoe. She nodded almost invisibly then said aloud, "I'm okay."

He nodded back. Message received loud and clear. His own pulse dropped to a low, steady thrum. There was no room for emotion.

Only to do what needed to be done. "We're going back to the camp-site until you feel better. I'm going to load the packs and then help you into the canoe."

As he picked his way up the rockfall to retrieve the packs, Rakmen ran through everything he could remember from the first-aid and CPR classes his dad had insisted that he take. Leah could be wrong about her ankle. If they rested a few days and then taped it up, she might be able to walk. He could make her a crutch and double back to carry her load as well as his own.

All those options evaporated as he finished loading the canoe and turned back to Leah. Her foot hung completely the wrong way, and the swelling had pushed the skin of her ankle outward until it looked like it might burst. It was an angry, reddish-purple, like an overripe plum. His stomach turned over as he sat beside Leah and pulled off his own boots.

"I'm going to help you into the canoe," he said. "I'll lift you and then wade in alongside it and set you in the middle."

He prayed he could do it without flipping them.

Leah exhaled in a long, controlled breath. "I'm ready," she said, looping her arms around his neck. She trembled like a child, and the slick smell of fear rose from her. Rakmen slid one arm around her back and the other under her knees, ignoring the discomfort of being so close.

He stood as gently as he could. Even so, her head wobbled against his shoulder, and he thought she might pass out again. Each step toward the water squeezed a gasp out of her, and she clutched his neck more tightly. He felt his way with bare toes along the slick rocks at the lake's edge until he stood beside the canoe. Water lapped at his thighs, cold and insistent.

"Brace as hard as you can," he told Jacey as he eased Leah onto the pack in the center of the canoe. The canoe tilted toward him, the gunnel dangerously close to the water, but he pressed one thigh against the underside of the canoe and steadied it. Leah kept a white-knuckle grip on the gunnels, panting hard. Rakmen scanned her face.

If she passed out in the canoe, they would go over in a flash. Scenes of what could happen then in deep water, with her unconscious, flickered through Rakmen.

Not that.

Not in the water.

"Can you stay awake?"

She gritted her teeth and nodded.

As quickly as he could, Rakmen helped Jacey into the bow and regained his place at the stern seat. The smell of wet was stronger now. It was already drizzling at the trapper's meadow, and Rakmen could see a hazy, gray line of rain pushing toward them. "Okay, Power. Back to camp. Full speed. We gotta get that tarp up."

Jacey hunched into the wind and dug in with her paddle. Rakmen set a course back to the campsite they'd left an hour ago. He'd thought they would be well away from Allard Lake by now. Away from the ghosts that haunted it. Turns out the past was way too hard to shake.

Gravel crunched under the bow of the canoe when they landed. The impact sent a tremor through Leah, but she didn't cry out. She waited, breathing hard, while he and Jacey got out. Once more, she wrapped her arms around Rakmen's neck and let him carry her up to the fire pit, where he set her down in front of the cold ashes.

Rakmen waited for her to tell him what to do, but she only stared at the fire pit, hands limp in her lap. Jacey stood on the flattened grass where her tent had been the night before, shifting her weight from one foot to the other and chewing on her hair.

He pulled his match case out of his pocket and tossed it to Jacey. "Start a fire."

She scraped a match on a rock and teased the flame into a pile of birch bark, dry pine needles, and twigs. A red glow illuminated her face. He carried the packs to the fire pit, pulled the canoe out of the water, and began setting up camp. Each task familiar after so many days on the trail, a reassurance that he would know what to do next.

He pitched the tarp first, draping it over a centerline strung between two trees and then pulling the corners taut. The tarp's leading edge was outside the fire pit. The bulk of it covered the log where Leah was sitting and then angled down to break the wind coming off the lake. As he tied the last knot, the rain reached them, pattering on the tarp.

The fire was roaring now, fueled by the huge pile of wood he'd cut the previous day. Leah and Jacey sat beneath the tarp, their bodies inclined toward one another, Jacey's head on her mother's shoulder.

Rakmen pulled one of their sleeping pads out of the pack and made a place for Leah to lie down. He slid Jacey's small pack under Leah's leg to elevate her ankle. He put a pot of water on the fire to boil. "Find the cocoa," he told Jacey. "It's in my pack."

One by one, Jacey unloaded the various containers of food, lining them up on the log. Rakmen unpacked their cook kit and spooned cocoa into cups. When the water was hot, he used a bandana to protect his hand and filled each one to the rim.

Raindrops tapped out a steady rhythm on the tarp and sizzled when they hit the flames. The lake's surface was dimpled gray. The trapper's meadow was a hazy line of green in the distance.

"What are we going to do?" he asked.

It took Leah forever to meet his eyes. When she did, it was like the first night at Promise House when he saw her through the ancient, wavy glass in the door. She was vague around the edges, lost all over again. "I don't know."

"We wait," he suggested. "Someone might find us."

Leah stared at him like he'd flunked one of her biology tests. "We haven't seen anyone on the trail for days."

"We'll rest your ankle until the swelling goes down. If I take your pack, we can make it out."

All of them looked at the ankle. Leah's toes were tiny protrusions on the bloated lump. It hardly resembled a foot at all. Rakmen tore his eyes from the injury.

He took stock as if seeing for the first time what was right in front of him. Their pile of gear was small enough to fit in the trunk of a car. The canoe, thin-skinned and delicate, could be destroyed with one hard kick. He and Jacey and Leah were fragile bodies, dragonflies buzzing the surface of the world.

Risk was everywhere.

The truth of it slapped him across the face.

Cell phones and ambulances and good intentions—even love—hadn't been enough to save Dora or Jordan or any of the kids in the Promise House memory book. Locking Molly in her house all summer wouldn't keep her safe. All the headlines he'd jotted down, which were supposed to remind him to expect one suck-ass thing after another, did not prepare him for anything. He couldn't hunker down and avoid more tragedy.

It would come.

Or it wouldn't.

Every second of every day, he was *au large*, hurtling into the unknown.

"I'm going for help."

Leah met his eyes, calculating his chances. "I can't let you do that."

"It's the only way."

Au large was carrying him forward like a tidal wave, and he knew he would try to ride it as surely as he knew it would knock him flat.

Finally, Leah spoke. "You're right. It is the only way."

Rakmen began dividing their equipment. Talking about it any more would immobilize him. He clung to the reassurance of their gear, each piece designed to keep them alive. He'd need the tent, slick under his fingertips, and a sleeping bag and pad because they were four days from anywhere. Ninety-six hours. Three nights alone. He couldn't think about that. He took the small aluminum pot. One plate. One spoon. His knife. He found his clothes bag and pulled out dry pants and boxers.

"You'll need this," said Jacey, handing him the folding saw. She gazed up at him, chewing on a piece of hair.

He took the saw and flicked the lock of hair with his finger. "Don't let Edna see you like that."

Jacey spit it out. "I don't want you to go."

Rakmen knew that look. She was about to cry. "I know."

"We're supposed to stick together like a team."

His throat tightened. If he cried, she would, and they'd be stuck. Really stuck. He had to turn the canoe. "We're still a team. You're still the power. Always telling me what to do."

Her chest heaved. The sobs were coming.

Leah shifted up on one elbow. "Hey Jacey, it would be good if we had more birch bark for the fire. Can you go find some?"

Jacey fumbled with her jacket pockets, staring at him with wet eyes.

"Go on," he urged. "Help your mom out. Team job. You're it." He pulled up her hood against the rain and sent her off.

Once she was out of earshot, Leah called to him, low-toned and urgent. "You need to take her with you."

His hands froze on the edge of the pack. If Jacey came, he wouldn't be alone. But that was just another failure. He was thinking of himself. Again. Rakmen bit the inside of his cheek. If Jacey were with him, Leah would be the one alone. And besides, a person like him couldn't be trusted to keep Jacey safe. Not for four days in the wilderness.

He sat beside Leah, head in hands. "You'll need her to keep the fire going, to cook for you."

"You'll go faster with a bow paddler."

"Not on the portages."

Leah grabbed his arm and squeezed with inhuman intensity. "Listen to me. You can and you will. What if I get worse? Go into shock? Get an infection?"

"I can't." Rakmen was the trapped beaver, unable to swim with a half-severed paw. No one was safe with him. He tried to tug out of her grasp.

Leah held on more tightly. "What if I die and she's here alone with a . . . Oh, God," she moaned. "Take her."

Rakmen stopped trying to pull away.

In death, Dora's tiny body had been heavy in his arms. The person he loved most in the world was gone. It broke his heart open to remember. He never wanted Jacey to look into empty eyes, to touch slack cheeks, to feel warmth dissipate. He swallowed back tears again. He couldn't take her, but he couldn't leave her either.

"Please," Leah pleaded.

He dropped his chin to his chest and felt the damp drizzle slip down the back of his neck. He nodded and kept nodding, convincing himself that this was right.

"Thank you." Leah squeezed his arm. "Thank you."

This might be the most wrong thing he'd done yet. But—

He looked once more at Leah's mangled ankle. It was the only way.

Rakmen added Jacey's sleeping bag and pad. Another plate. Another spoon. Leah was going through Jacey's clothes when she returned, raincoat dripping and hands full of white, papery birch bark.

"What are you doing?" she asked.

"I'm pulling out some clothes for you," said Leah.

Jacey dropped the bark by the fire. "Why?"

Leah's voice was flat and a little too loud. "We've decided that you are going to go with Rakmen. You'll travel faster that way. Get back sooner."

Jacey shifted uneasily, looking between them, reading between the lines. "You need my help." The words came out jagged and choked.

"I'm going to be just fine."

The lie lodged between Rakmen's ribs.

A mask fell over Jacey's face. She acquiesced like a wooden doll, jerky limbed, the kind you press on the bottom and they collapse. Rakmen placed his hand over Leah's, covering her thin fingers. "We'll be back as soon as we can."

CHAPTER 28

Twenty minutes later, the canoe was packed for traveling light and fast. They were leaving almost everything with Leah. She was in the tent, lying on her sleeping bag. Her broken ankle was propped on a clothes bag. Pots of water were lined up at the door. Rakmen had dug a latrine for her at the edge of the campsite. She'd padded the blade end of her paddle with a rolled-up T-shirt held in place with duct tape to use as a crutch.

"You've got the map?" she asked for the third time.

Rakmen patted the cargo pocket of his pants. Instead of feeling the lumpy jumble of Jacey's collection, he heard the crinkle of the ziplock bag holding the map. He missed the weight of her things, which he had stowed inside a sock along with his notebook to leave behind.

"You know where to go?"

"He knows, Mom. He's the direction." Jacey was too eager to go, too hard-edged. Harder than he'd ever seen her, but he understood the wall she'd built. It was easier that way.

They would backtrack as far as Cedar Lake. To get to Pen, they would take a shorter, alternate route. After that, it would still take another two days to get to Vesper. Once there, they were heading straight to Edna, who Leah was sure could call in a float plane for help.

172

Rakmen smoothed the pocket holding the map, feeling the rectangle against his thigh. Edna. What he wouldn't give to be on her rickety old dock right now. Four days was forever.

He felt his breath quicken and forced himself to slow it down. Take one step at a time between here and there. Lakes and portages. Paddle. Lift. Carry. He knew how to do these things now.

He had to take that first step.

He had to find the trail and carry.

The canoe was ready. Leah had everything he could think of to keep her comfortable. The day had turned all crispy blue sky and puffy clouds.

"Let's go."

Stoney-faced, Jacey let her mother hug her. Leah murmured last words like a lullaby. When she released Jacey, her face was wet. "Do what Rakmen says and I'll see you soon."

Jacey pressed her camera into her mom's hands. "I'm leaving this for you. I took lots of good pictures for you to look at."

"And I have my book." Leah held up *Pilgrim at Tinker Creek*. "I'll be lounging around while you guys are doing all the hard work."

"Yeah, Mom. You do that."

Rakmen took Jacey's hand and led her to the canoe. They had to go, and go now, before he lost his nerve. Rakmen pointed the bow of the canoe toward the portage on the far side of the lake. He matched his paddle stroke to Jacey's, remembering the first night she'd been at Promise House.

A hundred years ago on the phone, she had said that she had a dream—a dream where he fixed things. And we were all okay, she'd said, but now they both knew different. You can never promise okay. Or if you do, it's a lie.

• • •

The rest of the day was both like and unlike their very first day on the trail. His body hurt, not because of soft skin and weak muscles, but because he and Jacey were pushing hard. Neither wanted to stop for more than a few minutes, but every time Rakmen paused to check the map and verify their course, he made them both eat something. While he crunched a handful of nuts or sucked at a piece of chocolate, he traced the line of lakes and trails that led to help.

"I know where we are. I know where we're going," he muttered to himself.

Miles clicked by.

Jacey hardly spoke—another thing that marked the difference from the first day. Only once around mid-afternoon, she said, "What do you think Mom is doing?"

"Reading."

They kept paddling and crossed another portage.

By the time the sun hung above the hills in the west, they were beat. Robotically, Rakmen lifted his paddle, reached ahead of himself, and pulled it back in a smooth J shape. Again and again and again, he stroked. It would be full dark in an hour. They had to rest soon, but when Rakmen thought of the coming night, he couldn't suppress a shiver.

In the bow seat ahead of him, Jacey's shoulders slumped. She'd hardly paddled for the last hour. His muscles had gone past ache and into burn. They had to rest. Adding flex to his J-stroke, Rakmen pointed the canoe toward the nearest campsite.

Exhaustion roared through Rakmen as he put the bow into the shore. Jacey didn't move, and he wondered if she'd fallen asleep. "Jacey, we need to unload."

"We can't stop," she said, pushing back from the shore with her paddle.

"We have to." He planted his paddle on the pebbly bottom and held the canoe in place.

"We're supposed to get help."

Help was the refrain that had kept pace with his paddle strokes and his steps on the portages. *Help, help, help.* Rakmen wasn't sure if it was a plea or a goal.

"It's too dark to keep traveling."

A tremble twitched through Jacey's shoulders, and her hand on the paddle went limp. She whispered into the rapidly chilling air. "I want Mom."

Rakmen gulped back his own rising tears. He wanted his mom too. Or Dad with his big grin and hospital scrubs. He didn't want to be the adult, but there wasn't another living human for miles and miles.

"Come on, girl," he said, the words as gentle as he could make them. "I need you to climb out."

On shore, Jacey held the canoe while he carried their two small packs to the fire pit. He returned, pulled the canoe onto the shore, and urged Jacey away from the water. His every instinct said to keep moving. "We're going to set up the tent, then we'll eat, okay?"

Jacey wiped her eyes on the corner of her sleeve. By now, the sun hung an inch above the horizon. Deep, rusty orange light bathed their campsite and made the surface of the water look like lava. It would be a clear night, and cold.

Rakmen handed Jacey her fleece jacket and warm hat. In silence, they set up the tent. Too tired to build a fire and cook, Rakmen pulled out a bag of jerky and a couple of granola bars. Taking Jacey's hand, he led her away from the shadowed edge of the forest and into the day's last bit of radiance.

As they ate on a rocky point, movement along the far shoreline caught his eye. Some animal. Another tremor of apprehension stole up his spine. Night was coming, and nothing but nylon would separate them from it.

The sinuous, dark shape loped along the water's edge.

"Look," said Jacey, finally noticing the creature.

For a second, it seemed to have vanished, but it reappeared in the water, swimming straight toward them and trailing a V-shaped wake of ripples. Jacey squeezed closer, and Rakmen slid his arm around her. Only the animal's dark head was visible, and then that too disappeared under the surface.

"What was that?" she asked.

"Dunno."

Both of them startled when the animal's head popped through the water with a splash and a snort twenty feet in front of them. It had a round face, twitchy nose, and long whiskers. It snort-growled again, and then sneezed.

"Otter!" Jacey squealed.

At this distance, it was unmistakable. Rakmen could even see the silvered fur around its muzzle. It broke into such a monologue of wheezing and grunting that they both laughed. At the sound, it stared at them, head cocked, like a disgruntled old man.

Farther out in the water, three more heads emerged, and the little grandpa swam to join them. The family circled each other, snorting and wrestling in the water. Rakmen and Jacey watched until they disappeared around a point of rock.

Jacey looked up at Rakmen, her face alight. "I wish I could have taken a picture of that."

"Me too."

"We'll remember, okay?"

"Every whisker."

They finished their granola bars and washed them down with cups of water scooped from the lake. The sun slid below the horizon, and everything around them turned monochrome. They picked their way back to the tent in near darkness.

"Do I have to brush my teeth?" Jacey asked.

"Nah." He knelt to unzip the mesh door of the tent. "In you go."

She scuffed her feet in the dirt. "Rakmen?"

He peered up at her. "Yeah?"

"I gotta pee."

He handed her the toilet paper and a flashlight and leaned back into the tent, opening the valve to inflate their camping mattresses. When he turned to grab the sleeping bags, he saw that Jacey was still standing a few feet away, staring at the little path that led into the woods.

"Go on," he said.

She shuffled around to face him, clenching the roll of toilet paper in both hands.

He sighed. They had a night to get through, and it started right now.

Rakmen zipped the tent and stood. "I gotta go too. Where's that flashlight?"

They followed its thin beam down the tiny path.

Their feet crunched on leaves and twigs, startling some small creature that skittered away in the surrounding dark. Mice, probably. Always the mice. Jacey stayed on Rakmen's heels as he swept the light from side to side looking for one of the large, wooden boxes that served as an outhouse for each campsite. Rakmen wedged the flashlight into a forked tree branch so that the box and the ground in front of it were illuminated. He pulled the lid open, handed her the roll of paper, and stepped outside the ring of light.

"I'm turning around, but I'm staying right here, okay?" He relieved himself into a bush, watching every shifting shadow in the forest around him.

Home had never felt farther away.

In the city, trees were mostly solitary. Some old, some new and planted in neat rows, and all engulfed by asphalt and apartments and strip malls. Here, he and Jacey were the intruders. The trees won hands down. As they retraced their steps, the forest pressed against him; whether threatening or reassuring, he wasn't sure.

Their little camp—tent, canoe, paddles, hanging pack—was the tiniest speck in all this wilderness. He hung the flashlight from a loop at the top of the tent. It swung in wide circles, illuminating the blue nylon. As he wriggled into his sleeping bag, he imagined the view from space. A half-dome of sky blue glowing between the black trees and the inky slickness of the lake.

"I miss Mom," said Jacey from the cocoon of her sleeping bag. Her voice was muffled, and he couldn't tell if it was because of the layers over her mouth or because she was crying again.

His throat grew thick. They should have stuck together. They should have waited for someone to find them.

No one was around to find them.

If anything else went wrong, no one would ever know.

Jacey was definitely crying.

"Girl," he said, rolling onto his side and pulling the sleeping bag away from her face. "You know what?"

"What?" she snuffled.

"Your mom is in her tent, in her sleeping bag, same as us," he said. "She's got that little lantern on, and she's reading."

The dark outside was even darker.

All he could do was keep talking.

"Remember that big cliff we paddled past on the last lake?"

"Yeah," said Jacey.

"I bet if you were up on top if it right now, you'd be able to see her tent glowing in the distance."

"Like a pumpkin?"

"Exactly. And you could see our little blue tent. Your mom is probably thinking *Jacey had better be asleep. She needs a good night's rest.*"

"No, she's not."

"She totally is. And . . ." He grasped for words. "And she's thinking *If Jacey doesn't brush her teeth, she'll smell like a moose.*" Rakmen plugged his nose and in a nasally groan said, "Phew! Moose alert!"

Jacey giggled.

"If you start smelling any worse, I might have to tow you behind the canoe tomorrow."

"I'll brush in the morning."

He lowered his voice. "When we get back, we'll tell your mom about the otters."

"They were really cute," she murmured.

"And at home, you can tell your dad about the moose and all the birds and show him your amazing pictures."

Somewhere in the soothing rush of his words, Jacey began to snore softly, like a purring kitten. Rakmen checked the zipper of the tent and turned off the flashlight, but sleep didn't come easily. The treetops hummed with insects. The lake lapped against the shore. He wanted the roar of trucks on Lombard Avenue or music from the party house at the end of his block. Those were sounds that filled up space.

The loons started up, their howls reverberating off the water. Branches cracked and broke. Much later, he heard an owl call from the far side of the lake. After a moment it was answered by another in the distance. This wilderness was big and expectant. He was nothing but bone and flesh and gristle.

And beside him was a little girl, asleep.

CHAPTER 29

Morning couldn't come fast enough. As soon as it was light, he climbed out of the tent. His mind looped through the series of tasks that he had to accomplish to keep them alive.

Don't fall.

Don't drown.

Don't get lost.

The weather had changed in the night. Clouds blotted out the sun. The air felt heavy in his lungs. All his thoughts were circular. Each *what if* led to another and ended up back around where he started. There was no getting off this ride.

A memory hit him hard. He'd been eleven when his dad had taken him to the decrepit amusement park near the river. Rakmen had begged for the Screaming Eagle, a ride that suspended you from a pincer-like claw and swung to the tops of the trees. As they'd waited in line, the thrill coursing through him turned sour, and the corn dog he'd eaten for lunch churned in his stomach.

He didn't want to do it. It went too high. It spun too wildly.

"Come on," his dad urged. "It'll be fine. You'll regret it if you don't go."

No, he wouldn't regret it.

Not at all. This was not for him, but they'd waited in line, inching to the front. If he backed out now, Dad would know he was afraid. As the shoulder restraints locked down on his shoulder, the tears started, only to be swept off his face by the force of the ride.

The scream of a loon on the wing brought him back to the lakeshore.

Jacey was climbing out of the tent, rubbing sleep out of her eyes and staring blearily around their camp. "What's wrong with the clouds?" she asked. "They look upset."

She was right. The underside of the cloud layer was bloated and dark. The vapor seemed more solid than air, roiling in slow, sick swirls.

Rakmen tossed her a bag of trail mix. "Eat. We've got to get moving."

She nodded, and in silence they packed the tent.

Four hours later, the threatening clouds morphed into full-on storm.

Rain pattered on the underside of the canoe as Rakmen portaged from Chèri Lake to Tiske. The moisture-filled air licked at him. As soon as he flipped the canoe off his shoulders, he was soaked. Jacey had dug out her rain jacket and had the hood cinched down so far that her face was nearly hidden.

Rakmen shrugged into his jacket before joining her at the water's edge.

Waves curled, crested, and broke against the rocky shoreline. As far as the eye could see, peaks and troughs fought each other across the surface of the lake. Rakmen's stomach ached. This was worse than the Screaming Eagle. Rakmen wanted to elbow out of the line.

But Leah was miles behind them and help was miles ahead.

Right in front of them were waves big enough to flip a canoe. He hadn't paid much attention when Edna had gone on about handling what she called "big water." Something about not getting broadside and making planned turns.

Jacey edged closer to him. "What do we do?"

An icy river sluiced down the neck of his shirt, and he longed to be warm and dry inside the tent. He looked at his watch and wanted to cry. It wasn't even noon. They couldn't stop because of rain. Leah was back there with a shattered ankle and only enough food for four or five days. They still had so far to go.

Rakmen fought the urge to hit the nearest tree.

Don't fall.

Don't drown.

Don't get lost.

He hung on to the lifeline of tasks.

"I'm hungry," said Jacey in a small voice.

At least he could do something about that.

"Let's have lunch," said Rakmen, flipping the canoe upside down and resting one end on a stump. "Come on." He crawled under the small shelter, pulling the packs in after. Jacey squeezed into the little fort. While they ate cheese and crackers, Rakmen rechecked the map.

"Where are we?" Jacey asked.

He pointed to the northern shore of Tiske Lake. The portage they needed was at the opposite end of the narrow oblong of water. It wasn't a big lake, but the wind surged up from the south, whipping the waves higher and higher.

The trailhead felt as far as the moon.

They could wait it out, but Rakmen had no idea how long the storm would last.

And Leah was counting on them.

"We've got to keep going," he said, talking himself into it.

"Okay," said Jacey, slumping against her pack like a teddy bear missing most of its stuffing.

Rakmen handed her another piece of cheese. "Hey, girl, I miss you jabbering at me."

She frowned at him. "Then how come you always acted like I bugged you?"

"Who, me?" he protested.

She turned away like he wasn't even worth looking at it.

"No," he amended. "You're right. I thought you were annoying."

Jacey swirled one finger in the puddle forming in the low spot between them. "But I don't now."

In fact, Rakmen realized, her chatter had carried him along the trail in the days before Leah's accident. The treasures she slipped into his pockets had given him a secret boost, and the way she constantly snapped pictures of ferns and flowers and weird yellow mushrooms made him notice the world like he was seeing it for the very first time.

"I like talking to you," he said. "You're the power, remember?"

Her expression slumped.

Rakmen handed her his piece of chocolate. "Eat," he said, touching her on the nose. "We can do this."

"You don't know that."

"Ouch," he said. "Ye of little faith."

She bit into the chocolate. "Well, you don't."

A renewed surge of rain pounded on the canoe. Water streamed down its sides, carving a muddy furrow in the ground under each gunnel.

"You're right. A whole lot of crappy things can happen, but we've become really good paddlers."

Her chocolate-smeared lips tilted up in a crooked sort of smile. "You know what I wanted most?"

"I'm not following you," he said.

"I wanted to be a sister. I wanted to be good at something. I was gonna be the best sister ever."

The rain was turning everything around them to mud, but all Rakmen could see was the nursery in Jacey's house and the things she'd saved. The list of names. That bit of hair. The sucky bulb for baby noses. Her pudgy arms clutching the box of ashes.

His own mother's pregnancy had been weird and off-putting. He had not wanted to notice her body changing like that, growing ripe and full. He'd avoided thinking of it so completely that when his father put Dora in his arms, she was a revelation.

Unlike him, Jacey had planned and dreamed and prepared, and she got nothing at all. No hello. Not even good-bye. She got scraps. And even these she clung to.

"You would have been a great sister. I know it."

She smiled at him.

"Jordan missed out big time."

Jacey nodded.

"We can paddle this lake," he said. "Bow straight into the waves. Don't stop for anything." Rakmen zipped her jacket to her chin and pulled the hood down low on her forehead. He helped her into her life jacket and cinched it down hard before securing his own. They squatted under the canoe and squinted out at the deluge.

"Ready?"

Jacey threw back her shoulders. "Ready."

"Okay. Let's do this."

Like a jackrabbit, she shot out into the rain. Quick as anything, Rakmen flipped the canoe and tossed in the packs. The canoe bucked and rocked in the waves, but Jacey managed to clamber over the thwart into her seat. When she was in, he held his paddle crosswise to the gunnels and crouched like a sprinter on the blocks.

Jacey held her paddle up, and he launched them into the storm.

The bow rose up the crest of the first wave and slapped down the other side. Spray flew up on either side of the canoe. Jacey paddled hard, and he matched her pace.

Speed was everything. He wanted them through these waves and off this lake. Already they were shipping water. Each crashing descent of the bow sent water over the side. It pooled at his feet, but Rakmen couldn't stop to bail. Paddling required everything he had. Unless the bow was exactly straight into the wind, it grabbed at the canoe, trying to swing them broadside.

They inched away from the shore, fighting both the wind and waves, which tried to push them back. If either of them stopped paddling for even a second, they lost precious distance. Don't look at the shore, Rakmen told himself. Only the next wave. That's all that matters. And the next. And the next.

Rakmen was soaked through every layer he had on. His hair dripped into his eyes, blurring the sky and lake into a roaring gray mess. The only points of clarity were Jacey's bright blue rain jacket, the golden wood of the canoe, and his own hands on the shaft of his paddle.

He paddled as if the lake were his enemy, and he had to beat it back.

He paddled in a rage against all that he had lost.

He paddled because that was the ride he was on.

The muscles in Rakmen's chest and arms trembled with exertion. He willed them across the water, ignoring the pounding fatigue, scanning the waves for the far shore. A million paddle strokes later, Rakmen caught a glimpse of green through the curtain of rain. Ahead of them was the yellow sign marking the portage. A renewed gust of wind threatened to push them back, but he dug in and drove the bow into shore.

They had made it. Almost as soon as he had pulled their gear into the protection of the trees, the wind shifted, and the rain began to slow. The thinning clouds were letting in hints of sunlight.

Rakmen shook the water out of his hair. "I will never join the Navy or the Coast Guard or Captain Hook's pirates or any other gang that sails the sea."

Jacey grinned at him, rubbing the cramped muscles in her hand. "But you make a good captain."

"I don't know about that," Rakmen said, but he smiled back at her.

A half an hour later, every remnant of the storm was gone. Sun streamed out of a blue sky dotted with sheep-like clouds. Steam rose from the ground and their clothes. They changed into dry socks and set off again. Already the exultant feeling of having made the dangerous crossing was fading, and Rakmen's urgency returned at double intensity.

There was still a lot of ground to cover.

Fifteen lakes.

Twenty miles.

Two more days.

CHAPTER 30

Jacey dropped her paddle on the gunnels with a bang. "We're lost, aren't we?"

"No," said Rakmen, staring first at the map on his thighs then at the maze of islands in front of them. He hated this lake.

On the bow seat in front of him the girl slumped. Her filthy T-shirt stretched tight across her back. "This sucks," she moaned into her kneecaps.

Some jerk-wad explorer who thought he was funny had called this Twisted Lake. On the map, it was a blue mess of bays, poking out in every direction like splayed fingers. The longest, the middle one, was definitely flashing him the bird.

For three days, he'd kept them on course, tracking their progress from lake to portage. The map was soft from folding and refolding. The paper was separating along the fold lines, tearing a little more each time he opened it. But thanks to quadruple checking, they'd gone right.

Until now.

Molly's instructions—*Don't get lost*—pounded through his head. What he wouldn't give for an intact GPS.

Or a Coast Guard helicopter.

Yeah, right. He had nothing.

On the map, the portage they needed was down the middle finger, which pointed southwest on the other side of a cluster of small islands. He scanned the rocky, tree-covered masses in front of them, trying to figure out if these were the right islands.

Leaving the map on his legs, he resumed paddling, betting that they would be able to spot the portage bay from the other side of the islands. "Come on, girl," he urged.

Jacey didn't move.

The canoe slipped between an island the size of a train engine and another five times as big. A few craggy pines clung to their tops, roots clinging to cracks in the rocky surface. He didn't know how they grew like that. There wasn't even real dirt involved.

"Rakmen?" She was still bent double, staring at the bottom of the canoe.

"Yeah?"

"I can't stop thinking about my mom."

The storm yesterday had probably barreled through the campsite on Allard Lake, tearing at the tarp lines and battering Leah's tent. She would have struggled to keep the fire going. Rakmen didn't know how bad an ankle break could be. His dad said people sometimes got infections and died really fast, but that was usually in hospitals, staph or something. The skin wasn't broken. Rakmen clung to that small good thing.

"The faster we get to Edna, the faster we get back. So paddle," he ordered.

Jacey huffed at her legs.

Amid thoughts of what might be happening back on Allard Lake, Rakmen's concern about their pace ballooned. Slugs would travel faster than they were. He swabbed sweat off his forehead with the bottom of his T-shirt. The canoe kept gliding forward when he stopped paddling to refer to the map again. Looking up, he caught a flash of yellow in trees ahead.

He peered at it, praying for a portage sign.

Come on. Come on.

The water in front of them swirled to life as a loon rose from the depths.

"Jacey," he whispered. "Look."

She lifted her head an inch. The bird's red eyes practically glowed. Rakmen held his breath. They'd never been this close to one before. It was unbelievable how perfect it was. The tiny lines of white on its black throat stood out like snow on ink. If Molly were here, she would draw it, capturing the way it seemed made of water as it dove.

After the loon was gone, he went back to searching the tree line. That was a yellow portage sign. He was sure of it. "There," he said, pointing down the bay. "That will get us to Fancy Lake and then to Pen. We're close."

She peered suspiciously over her shoulder at him. "Are you sure?"

"Pretty sure," he said, trying to convince both of them.

"What kind of a lake name is Fancy?" said Jacey, sitting up.

"Beats me. Maybe it's Barbie's lake."

She snorted and began to paddle.

"Posh ladies rent it out for tea parties." If he could keep her talking, they could keep moving. "You have to wear a ball gown to paddle it. Too bad I forgot my tuxedo."

Finally, his girl laughed—a weak, little giggle.

They made it to Fancy.

And paddled it.

Tuxedo-less.

Unloading the canoe at the portage to Pen Lake, Rakmen was beyond exhaustion, stumbling along in an out-of-focus, sleep-deprived hallucinatory state punctuated by explosive nerves that sent him scrambling to recheck the map.

"Come on, Jacey." He hauled her to her feet. "One more portage to Pen Lake."

"I'm really tired," she whined, as he helped her load up.

He'd been talking nearly nonstop about whatever random fluff seemed likely to keep her going, but the well was running dry. He cast about for something to distract them both. "On this portage, I want you to tell me everything you'd take pictures of if you still had your camera."

"I don't want to take pictures."

Rakmen shouldered his pack and threw up the canoe.

"Pretend pictures."

"What's the point?"

He urged her up the trail. "See any mushrooms?"

"No," she said, plodding in front of him.

"That's a cool fern," Rakmen said, pointing from underneath the canoe.

Jacey said nothing.

The map in his pocket crinkled as he walked. He wanted Molly to know that he was not lost. Not yet, at least. Eight more lakes.

Tomorrow—he clung to the word.

Tomorrow they'd make it out.

CHAPTER 31

Worry urged Rakmen on. He paddled hard down the length of Pen Lake and kept pushing. At least they were back in familiar territory now. Seeing the sign for the portage which would bypass the rapids and take them to Wrangel Lake was like seeing the Safeway in his neighborhood back home. What he wouldn't give for a basket of jojos.

Rakmen spread out the map. "Here's the deal," he said, showing Jacey where they were. "I think we should try to run these rapids."

Jacey frowned. "What do we know about running rapids?"

"If we portage around all of them, it'll take hours. When we started the trip, we waded up one, remember? And your mom said the upper section was navigable."

A tug-of-war played out on her face. "I don't know. It looks scary."

The top part did look scary. The stream from Pen Lake funneled through a steep, rocky slot and then widened into a channel dotted with exposed rocks, but it sure looked like there was room to get the canoe through.

"After that storm, we know a thing or two," he said. "It would save us so much time." Rakmen returned to the map. "If we run them, I think we could make it to Soulé Lake by tonight. That would mean we could be at Edna's by tomorrow after lunch." The thought of Edna sent a thrill through him. He couldn't wait to see that crotchety old woman lumbering around on her ramshackle dock. He could place his problems in her capable hands.

"Let's do it," Jacey said, cinching down her life jacket.

Rakmen tied in the packs. "Just in case," he offered, when Jacey got all deer-in-the headlights. "We're not gonna flip."

She kicked a rock with her foot. "Don't do that."

"What?"

"Lie."

Rakmen stiffened. "I'm not lying."

"You are! Just like that stupid woman at church who told my mom nothing else bad could happen to her after Jordan died."

Rakmen felt as if the wind had been knocked out of him. He'd met people like that too, the idiots who believed life had a grief quota.

"Adults always lie," said Jacey, "but you—you've never lied to me before."

He struggled to remain upright as all the lies people had told him came flooding back. *It's better this way. Everything happens for a reason. Your dad and I will be fine.* So many lies, and he'd plummeted slick-tongued right into one of his own. He had lied to Jacey, fallen prey to the delusion that lies were comfort. He'd lied not because he hated her but because he loved her.

Rakmen knelt in front of Jacey and squeezed her sagging shoulders. "You're right. I was bullshitting. We might flip. I'm gonna try hard not to, but we might. Let's make these knots really tight, okay?"

Appeased, she added extra knots to the ones Rakmen had made. Once in the canoe, they knelt on its bottom to get their weight as low as possible. Rakmen pointed them toward the drop-off.

"You don't need to paddle," he said. "Watch for rocks and give me directions."

"Okay," she said in a small voice.

"If it looks like we're going to hit something, do that bow rudder thing with the paddle that Edna taught you. The move that lets you make sharp turns."

A tremor wobbled through her shoulders. "I'm scared."

He stopped paddling, but the canoe slid forward anyway, already caught in the current. His breath came fast and shallow. They could still paddle back and change direction. Rakmen sucked in air, his fear laced with something else, something potent. There was no going back, only forward, missing limbs and all.

"Jacey," said Rakmen, "look at me. This is important." She twisted around, and he saw the bit of hair clamped between her lips. "We can do this. We've dealt with worse."

She wiped her eyes on her sleeve and nodded. "Okay, captain."

"Together, now," he said, propelling them into the slick tongue of smooth water at the top of the drop.

The canoe picked up speed.

Their surroundings melted away, and for Rakmen, there was nothing but dark wave and white foam and his hand tight on the paddle ready to rudder the safest possible course through the churning water. As they hit the drop, his stomach flew into his throat, and they plunged down.

Rakmen had wanted fast, and damn, but he had it. When the canoe leapt the foot-high waterfall at the base of the chute, Jacey screamed, and Rakmen watched, horrified, as the bow dipped nearly below the surface. Water threatened to spill over the gunnels. He willed the canoe to levitate. If they filled with water, they would sink. For another second, the water seemed on the verge of winning, but then the body of the canoe bucked beneath him, righting itself, and he hooted his relief.

"Look out!" Jacey yelled.

Rakmen ruddered hard, swerving around a rock. Jacey scooted them away from another moss-covered boulder, and Rakmen knew he couldn't lose focus for an instant. The current swept them along, and they rolled with it, twisting and turning in the central channel. The trees on either side whipped past in a blur of green. This was the speed he'd longed for since they'd left Leah, but now it terrified him.

It was impossible to pull out of the rushing current.

All they could do was ride it out.

"Go left," Jacey called, plunging her paddle in and pulling the bow away from a submerged rock. He stroked hard on the right, adding speed that whipped them past the obstacle. Farther on, the stream curved around a small cliff. The land on the other side flattened, and the channel slowed and widened. Rakmen was grateful for the chance to breathe and flex the tensed muscles in his hands.

"Are we through?" Jacey asked, panting.

"Not yet. See how it drops again up ahead?"

"We're doing good, huh?"

"Real good," Rakmen answered. It was true. He could practically see them ticking off miles, closer every second to help and home.

The smooth pool of water that they were crossing ended abruptly at a submerged shelf of rock. It stretched from bank to bank right under the surface. The stream poured over it in a smooth line. Between the drop and the flat water of the next lake he could see the final stretch of rapids.

This was it.

He and Jacey were ready when the canoe launched itself over the edge and into fast water. Waves surged around them, and the canoe gained speed. Spray rose and caught the sun. Rainbow-colored droplets exploded in fireworks around the edges of the canoe.

Rakmen pushed his paddle into a hard J, pointing them straight at the center of the deep water far ahead. A flash of something dark in the roiling water ahead sent warning flashes sparking through him, but he couldn't fathom what was out there. Nothing that could be a threat, surely.

Jacey screamed, "Tree!"

Her call cut through the roar of the water and the wind in his ears but made no sense. And then, as if grabbed by the claw-tipped hands of an underwater beast, a horrible scraping noise shuddered through the canoe. Rakmen felt something wrench at them from underneath.

The world flipped, and they plunged into the water.

Rakmen thrashed against submerged branches. They scraped

across his face and along his body. Water pummeled him, trying to pull him along with the current, but he was held fast. Opening his eyes, he saw stripes of white and dark, foam and wood. A great tree had fallen in the water. Its branches were a net, catching everything. He thrashed violently, and then he saw orange.

A foot below him, Jacey was stuck too. The strap of her life jacket looped around a broken branch. The current swept over her shocked face.

Panic raced through him.

Rakmen's body bucked in the current.

Holding tightly to a branch, he thrashed himself free, broke the surface, gulped air, and went back down. The current clutched at him as he pulled himself, hand over hand, toward Jacey.

His chest ached for air.

Another few inches.

He was there.

But now her face had gone slack, and the current sucked at her limp arms. Rakmen forced himself to look away from her face. Instead, he slid one arm inside her life jacket, behind Jacey's back, looping his hand up over her shoulder. Once he had a hold of her, he let go of the branch. The river sucked against him as he fumbled at the buckles.

Black shadows pressed on his peripheral vision. He needed air, and soon.

He pressed hard on the clasp, and the first one clicked open.

His hand slipped on her shoulder as the water sucked against his legs.

Click—the second buckle came loose.

Bubbles spun out of Jacey's nose.

Not this girl!

Water was filling his mouth, burning the back of his throat.

Rakmen squeezed hard on the final buckle, and the current swept them downriver and away. He'd never held onto anyone as tightly in his life. Together they burst to the surface, the two of them buoyed up by his life jacket.

Gasping, Rakmen rolled onto his back, flipping Jacey so she rested face up on top of him. He kicked to shore and pulled free of the water. On the bank, he rolled Jacey onto her side, slamming the palm of his hand against her back.

Again and again.

Jacey's body was loose in his arms.

Breathe.

He pounded her back, swallowing back terror.

Rakmen forced a breath of air into her lungs. Her chest rose with his breath then wilted. Another. Then another.

"Breathe," he cried, the word a strangled prayer.

The world collapsed in on him.

"Please, please, please—not her too," he moaned, rolling Jacey to her side again. Rakmen could no longer hear the roar of the water or see the sun streaming down around them.

He was desperate, plummeting into terror, when a violent spasm rocked Jacey's body. Suddenly, water gushed from between her lips, and she rolled over to vomit in the sand. Jacey's breath came in great, wheezing gasps, her bone-white cheeks flushing red. Rakmen clutched her to him, crying with his whole body in great, racking sobs.

A great flood of loss and fear, relief and resurrection broke loose within him.

The *what ifs* and the *what could've beens* poured out.

There was Dora and there was Jacey.

There was now.

CHAPTER 32

They leaned into each other and sat for a long time. Rakmen's entire world was Jacey's respiration. Each inhalation a gift. Each exhalation a promise. Slowly, his perceptions expanded. His own breath came slow and steady. Rakmen could see the pulse in Jacey's wrist, the twist of the grasses near their feet. Water dripped from their sodden clothes. The river gurgled and splashed. In the deep hole where the tree was lodged, flashes of orange were visible in the swirling depths.

As he stared at the spot where the entangled life jacket twisted in the current, he realized he wasn't angry anymore. Not at Dora for leaving him in the wreckage. Not at himself for being unable to see what was breaking down inside her. He had been the best brother he knew how to be, and he had held her while she passed.

He squeezed Jacey a little closer.

"Rakmen?" said Jacey in a creaky voice.

"Yeah?"

"What about the canoe?"

Launched by another surge of adrenaline, he vaulted to his feet, racing the river downstream. He crashed through the brush, cursing like a madman and oblivious to the welts rising on his legs and arms.

If the canoe was gone or busted up—

Rakmen caught his foot on a root and went down hard. The pain slicing through his shin rebooted some circuit in his brain.

Don't fall.

Don't drown.

Don't get lost.

He had to stay focused. They were balancing on the knife edge.

Rakmen hauled himself up slowly. The shin would bruise but that's all. He looked upstream where Jacey sat, arms coiled around her knees, dripping wet. They hadn't drowned.

They had not drowned.

He picked his way downstream, alternately watching his footing and craning his neck to look for the canoe.

Around the next bend and at the bottom of the last stretch of rapids, he found it floating, mostly submerged, like a harpooned whale in smooth water fifty feet from shore. Tipped by the weight of the tied-in packs, it listed to one side, a single, curving gunnel above the surface. His paddle—intact—floated next to it.

Rakmen unlaced his waterlogged boots and swam out. Dragging the canoe back to shore turned his arms to putty. He could barely fumble loose the knots holding the packs to the thwart. Panting, he carried them to a flat, grassy patch of bank and returned to the canoe.

"Is it ruined?" Jacey asked, coming up beside him holding her broken paddle, retrieved from the rocks alongside the river.

He ran his hands along the canoe, checking for damage. Near the brass plaque that said *Au large*, his fingertips hit splintered wood, and worry surged through him, but as far as he could tell the cracks were above the waterline. The canoe had probably smacked a rock when it was upside down.

"It'll get us home," said Rakmen. "How's your paddle?" Jacey held it out. The blade had cracked, splitting off a section from one side, but it was still useable. Jacey stared blankly at the ground, arms limp at her sides. Stringy bits of green algae clung to her clothes.

"Come over here," he called, unbuckling the top of his pack and pulling out a soggy sleeping bag. "We've got to get this stuff dried out a little."

She didn't move.

"Jacey? Are you okay?"

She turned toward his voice, looking dazed. "Rakmen—"

"Yeah?"

"It's really easy to die, isn't it?"

He dropped the sleeping bag and went to her. "We didn't die."

Jacey crumpled before him. "Not this time."

"But—"

"No!" she interrupted, beginning to cry. "Don't say anything lame and stupid. Mom might be dead already." She slapped away her tears. "Jordan's dead! Dora's dead! All the ones at Promise House. It's what happens to kids. They get dead."

Rakmen crouched in front of her and held her shoulders. "Jacey—"

She mashed her lips together, daring him to lie to her.

"We didn't die. We're kinda broken. That's true. And you're right. It is scary, but we have to keep going. Broken bits and all."

She stared at him for a long time. He knew that look. She'd leveled it at him the first time they met in the front hall of Promise House. She'd seen something in him then that he didn't even know was there.

"And you know what?" he said, leaning in close. "We're a good team."

She touched her forehead to his. "Like brother and sister?"

"Yeah," he said, pulling her into his arms. "Exactly like that. Brother and sister."

CHAPTER 33

"This is it," said Rakmen. "The last portage."

After the accident, they'd made camp, both of them too drained to go any farther that day. They'd tossed and turned through a mostly sleepless night in their still-damp sleeping bags. Waking early, they'd broken camp and travelled fast all day. On the portages, Rakmen had to remind himself to be careful. He couldn't get hurt now.

By late afternoon, they were almost there. Vesper Lake was so close that Rakmen imagined he could smell the moose muck in the sludgy little bay. He couldn't wait for a nose full.

Uncle Leroy's fall-apart cabin waited for them.

Edna would know what to do.

Rakmen could rest.

Jacey laid her paddle across her knees as he guided them into shore at the end of Wren Lake. Sand scratched against the bottom of the canoe as the bow slid into the shallows. He patted the gunnels on either side. She was a good boat.

"Look," said Jacey, pointing down the shore into a patch of fragrant water lilies as she swung her pack on. A great blue heron, tall and long-legged, picked its way through the shallows without a ripple. Its plumage was a fluid glimmer of silver, but as the bird turned sideways,

Rakmen noticed the unnatural hump above the bird's left shoulder and the odd angle of its wing.

"There's something wrong with it," he said. "It's deformed."

The bird lifted one leg in the air and took another step forward, swinging its long bill side to side. The glare of the sun had turned the water into a mirror. It jabbed its bill at the unseen bottom and pulled it up again, empty.

The heron retracted its neck, cocking its head to look for prey again. The light was wrong. After a moment, the bird raised its wings, the right outstretched in a graceful arc, the left a bent twist of splayed feathers.

"What's it doing?" Jacey asked.

Everything about the way the bird moved looked painful, an ache matching the one in Rakmen's own shoulders. Maintaining the awkward stance, the heron stepped forward. In the shadow of the bird's body, the bottom of the lake was visible.

Rakmen understood all at once. "Smart bird. It's making shade with its wings so it can see the fish."

Jacey headed down the trail.

He needed follow her. Rakmen knew it. The faster they got to Edna, the sooner Leah would be safe, but he was filled with a fierce desire to see the mangled bird succeed in the hunt.

Rakmen kept watching.

After a frozen minute, its head and neck shot forward like an arrow. The crippled wing contorted violently, but when the bird settled, Rakmen saw a minnow twitching in its bill.

The heron flipped the fish head-down and swallowed. With a reverberant, gurgling croak, it rose into the air, held aloft by that twisted wing, and sailed over the trees toward Vesper. Rakmen grabbed his pack, threw the canoe to his shoulders, and followed it home.

• • •

When they entered the main portion of Vesper Lake, they could see Edna in overalls and an old fishing hat, casting a bobber into the weeds. Jacey tucked her paddle into the canoe, cupped her hands around her mouth, and screamed her name.

"Keep paddling," said Rakmen. "We're too far away."

Jacey yelled again, and this time, the squat woman turned toward them.

"We need a plane," Jacey called.

Edna squinted at the sky. "It's not going to rain."

"A plane!" Jacey, a ball of nervous energy, bounced up and down in her seat, sending ripples out from either side of the canoe. Rakmen paddled harder, sending them skimming into the dock. Milled lumber, metal nails, motorboat tied to one side—civilization. They had made it back from the middle of nowhere. Rakmen forced himself to release his grip on the paddle shaft. No more J-stroke. No more portaging. No more sleeping on the ground.

"Where's your mom?" Edna asked, catching the bow and pulling them alongside the warped dock.

"Hurt bad. There was a storm and rapids and we gotta go. Now, now, now." Jacey was breathless with hurry.

"Whoa, horsey," said Edna, helping Jacey out of the canoe and fixing an eye on Rakmen. "Tell me normal."

"It's true. Leah's stranded on Allard Lake with a broken ankle. She sent us to get help."

Edna frowned. "Allard is four days' hard travel from here."

"Yeah," said Rakmen, flexing his stiff fingers. "We know."

"You've been on the trail alone for four days?"

He nodded.

Jacey clutched at Edna. "Mom said you could get a plane."

Shock washed over Edna's face. Then she jumped into action. "Get the canoe on the dock and come up to the cabin. I'll get Coop on the radio. He's been flying fire patrol all day." She checked her watch. "It's nearly six. He may be at the hangar already. I hope he hasn't gone home."

Worry exploded in Rakmen's stomach. They had to get to Leah tonight. He couldn't bear knowing she was out there alone. Not when there were beds to sleep in. Not when he and Jacey were safe.

The crackling static of a CB radio filled Edna's tidy cabin. She waved them in and pointed toward a box of Nilla wafers on the counter as she established a connection. "Hey Coop," she said, "where you at?"

"Just heading in for the night. What's up?"

"We need an airlift. There's a woman hurt on Allard. Her kids trekked in to get help."

"That's at least four days out. You say they're kids?" The pilot's disbelief echoed through the radio.

"That's what I said. Can you pick them up at my place on Vesper? Her boy can lead you in."

"Will do."

"Good. See you in a few." Edna ended transmission with a stubby finger and turned toward them. "You kids—" she began, shaking her head. "Look what you've done." Her wrinkled face crinkled into a grin. She beamed at Rakmen. "Look at what you've chosen."

·   ·   ·

They heard the drone of the plane before they saw it, and went down to the dock to wait. The bright yellow float plane circled once and landed in a spray of water, coasting toward Edna's dock.

The pilot opened the door, counting heads. "Edna, I've only got room for three besides me. If we're bringing the woman back, one of you has to stay."

"Take the kids. I'll get an ambulance to meet you at the hangar." Edna nudged Rakmen and Jacey toward the plane.

They strapped in, and Coop took off down the lake in a roar, skimming the treetops and turning north. Rakmen pressed his forehead against the cool glass. Below, the rolling hills and shiny lakes looked more like the greens and blues on his well-worn map than the terrain they'd actually covered step by step and stroke by stroke.

He rubbed his calloused hands, proof that they had crossed all those miles by themselves, by sweat and tears. The distance that had taken them four days to traverse melted away in minutes. He could hear Jacey in the copilot's seat naming every lake, and Coop, stunned that a little girl would know the landscape so well, saying *yeah* to everything.

When Allard Lake came into view, Rakmen leaned forward. He could see the rocky point where they'd left Leah. From the air, her tent looked like a pumpkin amid all the green. Sunlight glittered on the surface of the water.

They were close now.

Coop would land the plane.

They'd get Leah and get out.

"Alright," Coop said. "I'm setting her down."

Only a few minutes more and he could walk away from being brave and being strong. As the plane descended, Rakmen could see the fire pit, a gray circle of ashes.

There was no smoke.

Nausea swept over him.

There should be smoke.

Rakmen had pushed himself past every challenge. He'd pulled Jacey from the water. All Leah had to do was keep putting sticks on the fire.

There should be smoke.

The plane touched the surface of the lake and skimmed toward the campsite. Coop shut off the engine, and the plane slid to a stop a hundred feet from shore. He opened the door and climbed down on the float to untie the canoe lashed there. Jacey leaned out of the open plane, peering at the shore. Rakmen unbuckled and stood beside her, scanning for movement.

A breeze rippled across the tent.

Behind them a loon wailed, its loud tremolo piercing him.

"Mom?" Jacey called.

Nothing.

Coop lowered the canoe to the water.

Jacey's call rose to a shriek. "MOM!"

An icy, electric current snapped through Rakmen. His pulse stuttered. Breath caught in his lungs. He closed his eyes against the blackness coming. Jacey dug her nails in his arm, gulping air. They had come so far together.

To have it end like this was more than he could bear.

He wanted to die.

No, that wasn't right.

What Rakmen wanted was to live. Not to forget or walk away or even heal. He wanted to keep going, wounds and all. Beside him, Jacey trembled and pressed closer. She sobbed, and the sound penetrated to the very center of his own throbbing wound. Rakmen slowed his breathing, preparing himself to open his eyes and face what they would find at the campsite, but before he could, Rakmen felt the change in Jacey. The tense current of her body shifted.

"Mom—" Jacey whispered.

But this time—

This time, her voice was buoyant.

He opened his eyes as Leah unzipped the tent door and waved at them.

Rakmen's every sense exploded outward. The stretching sky. The glimmering lake. The humming air. The world was expansive, vibrating, pulsing. And Dora was there, entwined around his heart. Her absence aching. And it was all connected.

Everything.

A unexpected longing filled Rakmen to stay right here. He knew the song of the wood thrush and the way a moose grazes on lilies. He could tell the difference between an otter and a beaver from the ripples they left in the water. When a loon rose to the surface beside his canoe, he knew to rest his paddle across his knees and watch in silence until it dove again.

He had found his way along these trails and lakes.

This place was where all the pieces had come together.

He wanted to stay, but he couldn't.

Up ahead, Rakmen could see the start of the next portage.

It was time to load up and go.

EPILOGUE

When they got back to Portland, it took Rakmen a week to get used to light switches and flush toilets and his dad being gone. His parents were working on things. That was good. They hadn't fixed things yet, but they were trying.

Rakmen turned sixteen and got his driver's license the same week. Also good. He drove to Ray's to see his dad, and he took Molly to the Alberta Street Fair. When they stopped to watch men on tall bikes juggling fire, she slipped her arm around his waist and leaned close, smelling like strawberries and the best parts of summer.

After dinner on the second Saturday in September, Rakmen asked his mom if he could borrow the car. "I need to go to Promise House."

"One last time, *mijo*?" she said, handing him the keys.

"Yeah," he said. "One last time."

"If you need the Kleenex—"

"—it's on the top shelf. I know Mom."

She smiled at him, a real smile, and he thought she was beautiful, like a piece of sea glass with the sharp edges worn away. "Take your time and drive safe. I'll be right here."

* * *

A low hum of conversation came from the parlor. Rakmen didn't know what group met on Saturday nights, maybe Alcoholics Anonymous. It didn't really matter, as long as the basement was empty. As he crossed the foyer, his sneakers squeaked on the wood floor, and Rakmen knew that, for him, the terrain of grief would always smell like lemon polish and sound like the whoosh of a tissue being pulled from a box.

At the top of the stairs, Rakmen flicked on the light. The long fluorescent bulbs flickered and clicked, slowly coming to full brightness. Nothing here had changed—same shag carpet, same ugly couch. Hand-me-down toys were piled in one corner. Cheerios were crushed into the rug. The smell of mildew filled his nose.

Rakmen opened the cupboard on the far wall and pushed aside stacks of colored construction paper and watercolor boxes. When he found the memory book, he set it gently on a battered card table and very slowly turned the pages, studying the faces of the dead.

When he reached the page Jacey had made for her brother, Rakmen paused, taking in the baby's closed eyes and unnaturally dark lips. When he'd last looked at Jordan's picture, he'd seen only the absence of life. Now he saw Jacey's features in the newborn nose and round cheeks. A rush of love and loss for the tiny boy filled Rakmen.

Leaving the binder open, he reached into his pocket and pulled out the photograph of Dora that he had chosen. In it, Rakmen held her so that they were almost nose to nose. Her downy head filled his palms and the curve of her body pressed against his forearms. He could smell her milky breath and loved the way she watched him with eyes full of stars. Her skin was whisper soft as he brushed his lips against her cheeks.

"I don't know where to start," he said, as he pasted the picture on the last page of the memory book. "A lot happened this summer. But maybe you know that. Leah's ankle is healing up. Jacey is as wacky as ever. Some of the photos she took this summer are on display at a coffee shop, if you can believe that."

Rakmen reached into his pocket again.

He held up a smooth, heart-shaped rock the color of cinnamon.

"Jacey found this on our trip. It reminds me of you."

He brushed his thumb across its smooth surface. "They invited me to go back next summer, to spread Jordan's ashes on Allard Lake."

He tucked the stone back into his pocket. "I'll keep this safe. Until next summer. Then I'll take it to Allard."

Rakmen was full up with a swirl of emotions.

Love and loss, fear and hope—

They eddied through him, a current carrying him into the future.

The last thing Rakmen did before closing the book was place his pen beneath his sister's name and write—

Au large.

ACKNOWLEDGMENTS

Books are hard to write, especially ones like this that are wrenched from the center of a very deep wound. All along the way I was buoyed up and cheered on and urged forward by an extraordinary circle of people. I am so grateful.

My family, Seth, Fisher, and Beryl, join me on every adventure, make space for my creative work, and always challenge me to be my best self. They are my safe place, my joy, and my everything good.

My parents, Marilynne and John, taught me to carry a canoe and paddle stern and count crackers and work hard. Because of them, I was lucky enough to know wilderness as a child, a gift I have tried to pass on to my own children.

My dear friends, Rebecca, Carrie, Chrissy, and Heather, have been there every step of the way, commiserating, conspiring, and celebrating with me. Shared loss brought Kristen and Mari into my life. Their support and understanding got me through many dark days. Jackie was there at the beginning, a life line.

My writing group, the Viva Scrivas, understood my vision for this book, read and reread chapter after chapter, and reminded me not to let the mother take over the story. My agent, Fiona Kenshole, took this manuscript when it was a half-finished mess, saw the beating heart of the story, and told me that I really must finish it. My editor, Andrew Karre, has a deft and subtle pen. At every turn, he pushed me to go deeper into the most painful parts of the story. It is a truer book because of him.

The team at Carolrhoda Lab and Lerner Publishing have been amazing. They made this writer feel like a super star at every turn. I also want to thank Ron for offering his expertise on fractures, Renee for fixing my Spanish, and Eric for translating the French.

Most deeply of all, I am grateful for Esther Rose. She changed everything.

ABOUT THE AUTHOR

Amber J. Keyser is a former ballerina and evolutionary biologist with a master's degree in zoology and a doctorate in genetics. As a research scientist, she studied evolution in western bluebirds, blue grosbeaks, marine copepods, and fruit flies and published extensively in the scientific literature. Now she writes both fiction and nonfiction for young adult readers. *The Way Back from Broken* is her first novel.